A MAN LIKE MATT

BROTHERHOOD PROTECTORS WORLD

MALLORY KANE

Twisted Page Press LLC

A MAN LIKE MATT

BLACK HILLS BROTHERHOOD BOOK #1

Mallory Kane

Hot SEAL Bachelor Party (SEALs in Paradise)

To Michael, whom I love.

ACKNOWLEDGMENTS

I'd like to extend a special thanks to my editor,
Angela Hoffman, who, thank goodness, is a
punctuation expert and a grammar goddess.

PROLOGUE

COLD RAIN HAMMERED the white roses that blanketed Will Vick's coffin, turning them yellow and soggy. The canopy the funeral home had optimistically placed over the grave flapped and creaked in the wind. A dozen or so people had braved the early April weather to attend the graveside service, but Black Hills Search and Rescue Specialist Matthew Parker had eyes for only one—Aimee Vick, his best friend's widow.

From his vantage point, several dozen feet away and partially hidden by trees, Matt could barely see the strands of brown hair that had escaped to blow across her pale face. Aimee didn't seem to notice. She stood stiffly, her arms folded protectively across her abdomen, nodding and smiling sadly as people filed by offering their condolences one more time before they headed home.

Matt pushed his fists deeper into his pockets and hunched his shoulders against the bone-deep chill that shuddered through him. A chill that had nothing to do with the cold April wind or the freezing rain that spilled off the brim of his Stetson.

Three days before, he'd done the two most difficult things he'd ever done in his life. He'd brought his friend Will's body home to Sundance, Wyoming, and he'd faced Will's wife and tried to explain how a weekend adventure had turned into tragedy, how, in the blink of an eye, she was widowed, and her unborn baby would never know his father.

Her utter shock and disbelief had been agonizing to watch, but he had needed to see it. Just like now. He needed to share her grief, her pain. More than that, he needed to take it away from her and onto himself, but he could not do that.

He saw Aimee wipe her cheek and bow her head for an instant. His eyes stung. He blinked and looked at his watch. He was out of time. His flight to the tiny border province of Mahjidastan was scheduled to leave in an hour. For a few seconds, he debated whether he should speak to her. But he quelled the notion as soon as it surfaced. If she saw him, it would only hurt her more.

He'd known Aimee nearly as long as he'd known Will, which was most of his life. He'd kidded Will about not deserving her. She was generous and kind, and forgiving to a fault. She gave everyone the benefit of the doubt, until they proved they didn't deserve it.

Three days ago, Matt had proven he didn't deserve her forgiveness. She hadn't said it, but the look in her eyes had told him more eloquently than words ever could. If not for him, Will would still be alive. If not for Matt, Will would be safe at home with his wife, awaiting the birth of their son.

Will's death was his fault.

CHAPTER 1

FORMER AIR FORCE 1ˢᵗ Lieutenant Matt Parker stepped outside Irina Castle's ranch house, which was also the headquarters for Black Hills Search and Rescue, BHSAR, in Sundance, Wyoming, and headed for the helipad several hundred yards to the east of the front door. He lifted his head and took a deep breath of crisp, fresh Wyoming air.

The day before, for the first time in a year, he'd set foot on American soil, on Wyoming soil. He was home, where he belonged. He loved the Black Hills. Even though those hills had tried to kill him and his three best friends almost twenty years ago, he loved them. They sustained him.

For a year, he'd done his best to track down any rumors of Americans in the remote mountain province of Mahjidastan, which was located in a disputed border area shared by Afghanistan,

Pakistan, and China. His objective had been to find Rook Castle, Irina's husband. But ultimately, he'd failed, as had BHSAR specialist Aaron Gold before him. And now, as of a week ago, Irina had called off the search. As he circled the UH-1B helicopter parked on the lawn, Brock O'Neill appeared in the doorway of the hangar.

"Parker," he said as Matt approached. The terse greeting was typical of the former Navy SEAL. He held out his hand and cocked his head to get a better view of Matt—the only sign Brock ever showed that the patch over his left eye bothered him.

Matt shook his hand. "Brock. How're you doing?"

"Hmph. You?"

"I'm okay. Not thrilled at being called home by Irina. Deke in there?"

Brock gave a brief nod. "Watch out. Your buddy's in a mood." Brock broke the handshake and headed toward the ranch house. Matt suppressed a smile as he continued toward the hangar. For Brock, that had been a warm greeting.

When he stepped through the open door, BHSAR Specialist and former Air Force 1st Lieutenant Deke Cunningham was leaning back in his desk chair with his feet propped up, tossing a steel bearing from hand to hand and scowling. A small

TV was tuned to a morning news show, its sound muted.

"Hey, Deke," Matt said. "Playing with yourself?"

Deke's feet hit the floor and he set the silver ball on his desk. "That loser I just hired overtightened a bolt and ruined this ball bearing. Brock offered to take him out for me. I'm considering it." He stood. "How the hell are you?"

Matt laughed and took Deke's outstretched hand. The two leaned in and patted each other on the back. "Been a while. Your trip okay?" Deke asked.

"Uneventful, which is good. Can't say I'm glad to be back," Matt replied, nodding back toward the ranch house. "The whole place is as silent as a funeral home. I got in so late last night that I haven't seen Irina. How's she holding up?"

Deke shook his head. "She's trying to act like she's fine, but she's not. She's in bad shape." Deke wiped a hand over his face and then raked his shaggy hair back from his forehead. "She's in town this morning, talking to her accountant again."

"So it's true?" Matt asked. "All her funds are wiped out?"

Deke nodded. "All her personal funds. Damn Rook for not signing everything over to her when they got married. I'd like to kill him—" Deke stopped and clamped his jaw.

Matt snorted. "Too late. But it's not like he knew he was going to die."

"You don't think so?" Deke's brows lowered and his blue eyes turned black. "He spent his whole life stepping in front of bullets for other people. Don't you think he figured one would hit him sooner or later?"

"I don't get it," Matt said. "She's his wife—his widow. Why can't she get his money?"

"It's the insurance company. All about the suspicious nature of his death. Just because they don't have a body—greedy bastards."

"Hang on. Listen," Matt said as he glanced at the TV. "Turn that up."

Deke scooped up the remote control and tossed it to him. "What is it?"

"Check out the pink dress. It's Margo Vick."

"Will's mother? Opening another Vick Resort Hotel?"

"No, look. That looks like an FBI agent standing next to her." Matt hit the volume control. "Listen. She's talking."

"—am personally offering a reward for any information leading to the kidnapper."

Kidnapper? Alarm pierced Matt's chest as Margo yielded the microphone to the FBI agent. Among the dark suits, her brightly colored dress drew all eyes to her.

The text on the screen identified the FBI agent

as Special Agent in Charge Joel Schiff. "We plan to hold press conferences on a regular basis, and we'll update the media as we have more information," Special Agent Schiff said. "Meanwhile, please let us do our job. Our primary concern is getting Mrs. Vick's grandson back home, safe and sound."

Matt gasped in alarm. "Aimee! It's Aimee's baby. He's been kidnapped." Matt stared at the screen, trying to absorb the truth of what Schiff was saying. The cameras pulled back to reveal the front of the Vick mansion, located just outside Casper, Wyoming. Besides the FBI agent and Margo Vick, several uniformed police officers stood on the marble steps, along with a couple of men in suits.

Matt stepped closer to the screen, scanning the faces. Then he saw her. Aimee was standing behind Will's mother, her face a pale blur. She was almost invisible, dressed in something dark that blended with the suits and uniforms.

"There she is." He didn't take his eyes off her until the camera switched back to Schiff. He rubbed his thumb across his lower lip as dread squeezed his chest. "There's more going on than just a kidnapping."

"What are you talking about?" Deke asked, glancing up at him, then at the television screen.

"This," he pointed at the screen, "is about me."

Deke turned to stare at him. "You've been out

there chasing ghosts too long. You're getting paranoid."

"No. Listen to me. About a month ago, my journal disappeared from my room."

Deke frowned and picked up the ball bearing again. He tossed it back and forth. "You mean your laptop?"

Matt shook his head. With every passing second, the pressure on his chest grew. "I keep notes in a leather journal just for my use. I write my reports to Irina from my notes. You know, rumors of Americans in the area, anything I can glean about what Novus Ordo or his terrorist friends are up to, lists of expenses."

"You can't find it?"

He nodded. "It was stolen. I know it."

"Okay. How does your missing journal have anything to do with the kidnapping of the grand-baby of one of the wealthiest women in Wyoming?"

Matt glanced back at the TV but there was a commercial on. He took a long breath. "Because I didn't just write work stuff in that journal." He turned toward the window, letting his gaze roam over the jagged peaks in the distance. "It's been a year since Will died, and I haven't talked to her."

Deke didn't comment.

Matt rubbed his lip. "I just couldn't face her. So, I was trying to compose a letter. A way to—tell her how sorry I am."

"I don't follow."

"Novus knows we've been searching for any clue that Rook survived the sniper attack. I was followed from the moment I got to Mahjidastan. Whoever stole my journal was sent by Novus, probably to see if I had any intel that would lead him to Rook. So now—"

"Now he knows how you feel about Aimee," Deke supplied. He set the ball bearing down on his desk and sat up straight.

Matt's first instinct was to lie, but his friend Deke knew him too well. "Yeah. Not only does he know how—how I feel, he knows I'm William's godfather. And now Irina has called off the search for Rook. What if Novus thinks she stopped because I found him?"

"And what? You think Novus had Aimee's baby kidnapped—"

"To get to me."

Deke shook his head. "I don't know, man. It's kind of a stretch. Wouldn't he have grabbed you before you got here to our secure compound if he thought you knew something?"

"Think about it. I've been in Mahjidastan for the past year searching for information about the only man on earth, outside of Novus's inner circle, who can identify him. And before me, Aaron Gold was there for over a year. There hasn't been a day since Rook disappeared off that boat that a BHSAR specialist hasn't been searching for him." He pronounced it *bee-sahr*. "Suddenly, Irina pulls me out and doesn't replace me. Novus didn't have a chance to get his hands on me. I left within four hours of Irina's call."

Deke gave a short, sharp laugh. "That's quite a conspiracy theory. But it's possible. So what are you going to do?"

Matt met Deke's gaze and set his jaw. "If Novus Ordo has taken Aimee Vick's baby to try and get his hands on me to interrogate me about Rook, I'm going to make it easy for him."

AIMEE VICK PACED BACK and forth across the living room of her mother-in-law's house. The entire place was crawling with FBI agents, uniformed police officers, and technicians working with computers and cell phones.

Aimee looked at the grandfather clock for the hundredth time—or the thousandth. Two thirty p.m. It had been eight hours. Eight terrifying, unbearable hours without her baby.

When she'd woken up that morning and discovered that William was gone, she'd hadn't believed she could survive one hour, much less eight, without him. But she was still alive, and still rational—barely.

William Matthew Vick was only seven months old, and Aimee had never spent a night without him. Hardly even an hour. He was her anchor, her whole life since her husband's death.

She didn't notice that someone else had come in the front door until she heard her name called. She turned and found herself face-to-face with Matt Parker, her husband's best friend, her baby's godfather, and the last man on earth she expected to see.

"Matt," she croaked. Her voice sounded hoarse and harsh to her ears. The last time she'd seen him was a year ago, when he'd brought her husband's body home. He looked every bit as stricken as he had that day.

Her first impulse was to hug him, but she didn't. Her emotions were already in turmoil, and seeing Matt ramped up her anxiety. She ought to be furious at him. He hadn't shown up for Will's funeral, nor for William Matthew's christening, even though she'd honored Will's request to name Matt as William's godfather.

She'd spent a good portion of the past year filled with anger. At Matt for taking Will skydiving. At Will for stupidly jumping out of a plane and dying. At herself for not putting her foot down and refusing to let him go.

Matt looked down and rubbed the back of his neck. After a few seconds, he raised his head enough to meet her gaze. "Aimee, I'm so sorry about your baby. I just talked with Special Agent Schiff. He's agreed to let me help with the investigation—if you agree."

Aimee clutched at her abdomen, where the hollow nausea that had been her constant companion ever since Will died was growing, threatening to cut off her breath. "How did you get here?" She shook her head. "I mean, it just happened—"

"It doesn't matter. I'm here. Will you let me help?"

Aimee looked at Special Agent Schiff, who nodded at her reassuringly. "I can't believe—I haven't seen you since—." She clamped her mouth shut. She wasn't making any sense.

Matt's gaze faltered. "I know. I'm sorry, Aimee."

Aimee jumped when her mother-in-law Margo laid a hand on her shoulder—a heavy hand. "Aimee, dear, why don't you get a glass of water?"

"I'm not thirsty." She tried to step away from Margo's grasp, but the woman held on.

"Aimee, get yourself some water. I'd like to speak to Matthew alone for a moment."

Aimee rubbed her temple where a headache was gathering. She knew what Margo planned to do. She was going to tell Matt to leave. She could practically see the wheels turning in her mother-in-law's head. A lot of people in Casper knew that Matt had been with Will when he'd died, and

Margo did not like the Vicks being the subject of gossip.

Appearances. They'd always been her mother-in-law's main concern. The magenta suit she wore attested to that. Only Aimee and the owner of Margo's favorite dress shop knew that her first act upon hearing of her grandson's kidnapping was to call the shop's owner and have the suit rushed over in time for the press conference.

"Anything you have to say, you can say in front of me, Margo." Aimee stiffened her back and met her mother-in-law's gaze.

"If you're sure, dear." Margo turned to Matt. "Aimee is terribly distraught. I'd rather she not be upset further. Perhaps you should leave."

Matt raised his brows and gazed at Margo steadily. "I have every right to be here. William Matthew is my godson."

A godson he has never seen, Aimee thought. To make matters worse, Margo had spent the year since Will's death trying to coax Aimee to relinquish control of William's future to her. *I know you understand that I have the resources and the connections, dear. You don't.*

Grief and fear and anger balled up inside Aimee, until she felt like she was going to explode. She had to bite her tongue to keep from lashing out at both of them. Aimee had loved Will, but the six years of their marriage had been a tug of war between him and his mother. She had been thrust into the middle, an impossible position. Now she was in the same position again, this time standing between Margo and Matt. "William is my child," she blurted out. "This is my decision."

Every eye in the room turned their way.

"Aimee," Margo said warningly as her fingers tightened on Aimee's shoulder. "Don't make a scene."

Aimee wasn't sure how she felt about Matt showing up after a year—almost to the day—since Will's death, but she had no doubt about his ability. As a weather expert and survival specialist, rescuing the innocent was what he did. If anyone could save her child, Matt could.

"If Special Agent Schiff agrees, I want Matt here. It makes sense for him to be involved. He's trained in rescue and recov—" her throat closed on the word *recovery*. "Rescue," she said, as firmly as she could. *No crying.* She hadn't cried yet, and she didn't plan to start now. Crying never helped anything. She was afraid if she started, she wouldn't be able to stop.

Margo's dark eyes snapped with irritation as she drew in a sharp breath. Then, with a quick glance around the room, she consciously relaxed her face and nodded. "Of course," she said stiffly. "I was certainly not implying otherwise." Her grip on

Aimee's shoulder loosened and turned into an awkward pat.

The ring of a phone split the air. Aimee jumped. It had to be him. *The kidnapper.*

She whirled, looking for her purse, and then remembered that the FBI had forwarded her phone to a line that was hooked up to a laptop. It rang again.

Special Agent Schiff motioned her over to the table where a technical specialist sat in front of the computer. "Mrs. Vick—" Schiff said in a cautionary tone. "Remember what we discussed?"

She had to talk to the man who'd taken her baby. Her stomach turned upside down. Matt moved closer. He and Schiff stood behind the techie, watching the laptop screen over his shoulder.

"Wait to see what he says," Schiff cautioned her. "Once he starts talking ransom, you insist it be delivered by a family friend—Parker. Don't let him bully you. Don't give in to any demands. You are in control, not him. Got it?"

Aimee had never felt less in control in her life. Her baby was in the hands of the monster on the other end of the phone, and she was being forced to bargain for his life.

"And remember, you and he will be on speaker. Quiet, everyone. On my count," Schiff said to the techie. "Connect the call on three."

She nodded jerkily. Her throat was too dry to swallow. Schiff nodded at the computer tech, glanced at Matt, then held up a finger. "One," he mouthed to her.

A second finger went up. "Two."

Aimee bit her lip. Matt stepped closer.

Schiff held up three fingers. "Three." He nodded.

The techie pressed a key and nodded to her. "Hello?" she croaked.

"Hello, Aimee," the voice was cold and menacing. "Hello, Special Agent Schiff, and whoever else is listening."

Aimee stiffened at the kidnapper's threatening tone. At the same time, Matt stepped close to her. He extended a hand as if to touch her, but he didn't. Still, his closeness gave her courage.

"Where is my baby?" she cried. "I have to know if he's okay."

"Your baby is perfectly safe for now," the harsh voice said. "It's up to you to keep him safe. Let's talk business."

"What do you want?" she asked tightly.

"Money, of course," the man replied. "Are you listening, Schiff? Because I will only say this once. I want two million dollars wired to a bank account in Luxembourg. Don't give me any problems. I know who Margo Vick is." The man's voice was cold and hard.

Aimee felt sick. She could hardly make sense of what he was saying. She took a deep breath, but before she could speak, the man continued.

"And no excuses about how much time you need, Schiff. Just do it."

"I have to talk to my baby first," she said. "He needs to hear my voice."

"Shut up. You're not giving the orders. I am. Now here's where the exchange will take place once the money has been successfully transferred." He rattled off some numbers that meant nothing to Aimee. Out of the corner of her eye, she saw Matt nod at Schiff.

"Got it?" the man snapped.

Schiff sent her a nod.

"Y-yes," she said.

"Tomorrow at 1500 hours. *Aimee*," he emphasized her name, "if you want to see your baby again, you will be there."

Beside her, Matt jerked. He shook his head fiercely at her.

"I—I don't know," she stammered, her heart stuck in her throat. She didn't remember what she was supposed to say.

"Family friend," Schiff mouthed.

"Wait. I can't come alone," she said as strongly as she could. "I—I'll need to care for William Matthew. I need to bring a—a family friend—"

"I don't care who you bring, as long as you

follow instructions. Schiff?" the kidnapper said. "What did I tell you? I will not say it again. Make it happen."

"Hang on," Schiff said. "Two million is too much and your location is too dangerous for Mrs. Vick. She can't navigate that terrain by herself."

"Then you'd better send somebody with her who can, hadn't you?"

Schiff glanced at Matt. "Oh, we will. But we're not transferring a penny without proof of life."

"Proof of—" Aimee stammered, looking from Schiff to Matt.

"Don't worry, Aimee," Matt said, pulling her away from the call. "William Matthew is all right. I promise you. They just want the money."

Aimee's throat closed and her eyes stung with tears. "Proof—" she whispered.

"Why is Schiff arguing with the kidnapper? He's going to make him angry," she said. "It doesn't matter how much money it is. Right, Margo?" She looked at her mother-in-law, but Margo's attention was on Special Agent Schiff, who was still talking to the kidnapper. Matt touched her arm. "Negotiating is part of it. Let's go into the other room."

Aimee pulled away. "No! I have to talk to my baby. He has to hear my voice. He doesn't know those people."

"Aimee, listen to me." Matt turned her to face him. "Special Agent Schiff knows what he's doing.

They'll work out the details. He won't agree to transfer any money until we have the baby."

Aimee saw Schiff walk away from the phone. She pushed past Matt. "Did he hang up? What about my baby? I needed to talk—"

But Schiff was talking to the computer tech. "Give me those coordinates," he said. "Parker, get over here. You said you're an expert in weather and survival," Schiff said to Matt. "Know where that is?"

"That latitude and longitude puts it north of Sundance," Matt muttered, checking his phone. "It's about halfway up Ragged Top Mountain. Rough terrain. Plus we've got a late winter storm building. Could dump a foot or more of snow before it's done." He turned to Margo. "Isn't Ragged Top where your husband's hunting cabin was? Will and I went up there a few times."

Margo nodded stiffly. "That's right. No one's been there in years. Why?" she asked, approaching.

"The kidnapper is demanding that we meet at a location on the south side of Ragged Top," Schiff answered her.

"South? That's—" Margo stopped, frowning. "Oh, dear." Her face drained of color.

"What?" Schiff demanded. "It's what?"

Margo blinked. "It's just so hard to get up there. Especially this time of year and with a storm coming. Why would they—I mean—you can't send Aimee up there by herself."

Aimee frowned. She had only seen Margo shaken a handful of times since she'd known her. What was bothering her?

"She's right," Matt said. "That's the south side. It's the steepest. It's pretty dangerous. Boss Vick had his cabin built there because he loved hunting in winter and because he always had to be the toughest son of a bitch in the valley." Matt's jaw clenched in determination. "I can do it. I've pulled innocents out of more remote locations than that. But this storm's coming in fast. By 1500 hours tomorrow it'll be right on top of that peak."

Schiff frowned. "The weather service said it would be moving into this area late tomorrow night."

"Yeah, that's what they're saying. I'm going in alone."

Aimee stiffened. She knew he could do it. That wasn't the problem. He was a search and rescue specialist, trained in the Air Force. There was no one more suited to the job. But the kidnapper had been very specific about her being there.

"Don't even think about leaving me behind, Matt," she said. "William Matthew needs me. I will be there to take him in my arms."

IRINA CASTLE SAT in her office, clicking the top of a pen over and over. She stared out the window at the view of the starkly beautiful Black Hills of Wyoming. Rook had built their house facing them. He loved those mountains.

"I'm sorry, my love," she whispered. "I tried as hard as I could to keep you alive." She stopped, her heart too full, her throat too tight to continue. She blinked and reached for a tissue just as her phone rang.

It was Hank Patterson, a former Navy SEAL who had founded a sanctuary for former military men and women transitioning from active duty to civilian life. He'd created an organization called Brotherhood Protectors that allowed the former members of the military to continue to be useful and protect those who needed them.

"Hi, Hank," she said as the ghost of a smile landed on her lips. "How are you and Sadie and Emily?"

"Irina, hello. We're fine. Really good. I called to check on you, though. I'm hearing a lot of chatter that I'm hoping isn't true."

Irina grimaced. It had been over two years since her husband had been shot on the deck of their yacht and fallen into the deep waters of the Mediterranean Sea. Authorities had searched for him for days before declaring him missing and presumed dead.

"Let me guess what the chatter is saying," Irina said. "After more than two years, Rook Castle's widow has called off the search for her husband, who, by all accounts, was shot and killed on the deck of their yacht and whose body was lost in the depths of the Mediterranean." She had to struggle to finish the sentence without her voice breaking, but she did it. She'd done it for more than two years. Kept her grief private while she showed a brave, determined face to the world.

"Almost word for word," Hank said. "The only thing you missed are the two different theories of why. Is this about money, Irina?"

She arched her neck and rubbed a sore muscle. "What was the other theory? That I stopped the search because we found him?" She laughed, not because it was funny, but because it was absurd. "We didn't find him."

"So it is about money. Why didn't you call me? I'd be happy to help you if you want to keep searching for Rook. I'll do anything I can. You know that."

"I do know, Hank, which is why I'm telling you no. I saw the bullet strike him. I saw the blood. I watched him tumble overboard and disappear." She swallowed, trying to take the tremor out of her voice. "It's past time I stop believing in impossible miracles. I couldn't save Rook, but I can save what's left of his dream."

"What's left?" Hank said. "What do you mean?"

Irina sighed. "I've depleted my personal funds and our discretionary income. I shouldn't have allowed the search to go on for this long. I've had to dismiss most of the ranch staff. The only people here at the ranch are Black Hills Search and Rescue specialists."

"Let me help. Please. I owe that to Rook."

"That's not how Rook saw it. He always said that he was able to realize his dream of his Black Hills Brotherhood because of you."

"Yeah, he was exaggerating about that. He told you we knew each other in school, right? We were good friends. He told me about Arlis Hanks, about how Hanks died saving them and how he wanted to establish a group of former Air Force specialists to pay forward what Hanks had done for him and his friends. I saw that Rook's dream of helping his brothers-in-arms meant as much to him as mine did to me. When I had to leave the SEALs and go back to my dad's ranch, it was hard. People like us live on the edge, with an expectation of danger around every corner and the knowledge that we could die any second. Going back to civilian life is a difficult adjustment. I wanted to find a way to help my friends, my brothers, make that transition. I approached Rook and let him know that I had a place for him and his team here, but his dream was to go back to the Black Hills. You know, in some small way, I think Rook's story may have influenced me." Hank paused, but Irina couldn't speak. "I'd be honored to help," he finished.

"You helped so much last year when you sent us Rafiq Jackson," Irina said after a moment. "He has turned out to be really good. Deke and the others are impressed, and trust me, it takes a lot to impress Deke."

"I've met Deke Cunningham, and I agree. I'm glad Jackson worked out for you. He impressed me, too. I don't guess you'd consider sending him back to me, would you?"

"No," she said, laughing. The laugh was genuine this time. "Next time, plan ahead. I tell you what,

Hank. If you'll let me, I'll call on you if I need you. How's that?"

"I'm going to hold you to that. And if I don't hear from you sometime soon, I'm going to call you again."

"It's a deal, Hank. Thank you. Please tell Sadie I plan to get over there to your Crazy Mountains sometime soon. I need to meet that adorable daughter of yours."

"I'll tell her. Luckily my daughter takes after my adorable wife."

"Thanks again, Hank. Bye." Irina leaned back in her office chair and rubbed her eyes.

"Irina?" It was Deke. He was standing in the open door of her office. "Are you okay?"

She sat up. "Sure, I'm fine. I was just talking to—"

"Hank."

"How long have you been standing there?"

"Long enough to hear that you think it takes a lot to impress me," he said with a wry grin.

"I don't think it. I *know* it."

"You mind telling me what Hank wanted?" Deke asked as he sat in one of the chairs around her desk.

"He's heard the chatter. He wanted to check on us, and he offered his help."

"Are you going to take him up on his offer?"

Irina shook her head. "No. We need to get back to BHSAR business, at least as much as we can."

"There may be something we need to do before that."

Irina frowned at him.

AFTER COORDINATING times and plans with Special Agent Schiff, Matt drove straight back to Castle Ranch. He needed to talk to Deke right away.

Deke was one of the most decorated Air Force Combat Rescue Officers alive. His skill with a rifle was legendary. The only thing he did better than shoot was fly a helicopter, which was exactly why Matt wanted him on alert for the ransom exchange.

When he got to the hangar, Deke wasn't in his office, so he went looking for him and found him sitting at the conference table in Irina's office, along with Specialists Rafiq Jackson and Aaron Gold. He nodded at Rafe and Aaron, acknowledged Deke with a brief glance, then turned to Rook Castle's widow.

Irina smiled and stood to give him a hug. She was as vibrant and lovely as ever. Her blond hair glowed in the sunlight that streamed in the window. But behind the sparkle in her blue eyes, he could see a shadow of grief.

He couldn't imagine how difficult it had been for her to give up searching for her husband. She'd watched as a bullet had hit him. Seen blood spurt from his body as he'd fallen into the Mediterranean Sea. Even so, she'd clung to the hope that because his body had never been recovered, he might be alive.

Now, she'd given up. For everyone who knew her, and who had supported her efforts to find him, that made it official. After more than two years, Rook Castle was dead.

"Irina," Matt said. "When you called me the other day, I didn't get a chance to say—"

She held up a hand. "I know. Thank you, Matt." Her smile turned sad. "It's been more than two years. It's time I stopped living in a fantasy world. What's important now is rescuing Aimee's baby. I saw a clip of Margo Vick from the news, and Deke has told me what he knows. I called to speak to Aimee, but I got Margo. She said Aimee was resting. Please let her know that if she needs them, all my resources are available to her."

He studied her face, wondering if Deke had told her about his theory that Novus was behind the kidnapping. He decided not to mention it. "Thanks, Irina. I know Aimee will appreciate it. I was hoping Deke could help me out."

"Of course. You two talk here. Let me know what you need from me. Matt, I am so glad you're back." She touched his shoulder as she headed toward the door. "I need to check with Pam about my schedule for today. Rafe, Aaron, walk out with me."

Matt watched them as they left the conference room. His gaze fell on the plaque that represented the organization Rook Castle had created. Black Hills Search and Rescue, Incorporated. The plaque was small and plain, with a simple message.

IN MEMORIAM
Vietnam Veteran and Combat Rescue Officer
Arlis Hanks, 1944-2000. Our pledge—to honor your
bravery by rescuing the innocent.

Matt walked over and touched the four signatures that were emblazoned into the bronze. Robert Kenneth Castle, Deacon Joseph Cunningham, Matthew James Parker, and William Barker Vick. Underneath were the words *Black Hills Brotherhood*. Then he sat and propped his elbows on the table. He intertwined his fingers.

"Did you get a chance to talk to Rafe? Did you ask him about Novus?"

"He's listening in on activity around the Afghan/Pakistan/China borders. Chatter's high in the region as always. Slightly higher since Irina called you home." Deke rubbed his face.

"I'm glad we've got Rafe. It's good to have

someone who speaks the language. What about Novus?"

"Well, you made big news when you left from over there. Rafe thinks you might be right. Either Irina called you back from Mahjidastan because she ran out of money or she stopped because she found Rook. He says most of the speculation is that you found him."

"Hmph. I wish it was true."

Deke didn't respond.

"What about you?" Matt asked him. "Are you on a case right now?" he asked.

"Nope. No case. Just hanging. I'd love to be out kicking butt somewhere, but I feel like I need to be here, you know?"

"Irina looks pretty good."

Deke shook his head. "It took a lot out of her to finally make the decision to stop searching for Rook. All this time she's lived with the image of him being shot, then disappearing into the sea. It was awful—" Deke's voice cracked. "I mean, it had to have been."

Matt didn't have to imagine. He had his own nightmares. His dreams were haunted by the sight of Will Vick spinning helplessly as he plummeted to earth, trailed by the parachute that failed to open.

"What about Aimee?" Deke continued.

Matt blinked. "Not good. And I'm afraid I made

it worse, showing up like that." Matt stared at his clasped hands. "The baby was kidnapped, and Aimee's about to break. I'm afraid the situation is pretty grave. FBI Special Agent Joel Schiff was there, at Margo's house, waiting for contact from the kidnapper. They have no idea who he is, and they couldn't trace the call. Schiff negotiated the caller down to one million dollars to be transferred to a numbered account in Luxembourg once we have the baby. The FBI will then try to trace the account while the transfer takes place. We're to meet them at a specific set of coordinates on the south side of Ragged Top Mountain. They won't even try to move in on the kidnappers until I get Aimee and the baby to safety."

"The kidnapper said the south side of Ragged Top? That's pretty rugged terrain. Isn't that where we went with Will and his dad that time?" Deke asked.

"Yep. That's where Boss Vick's cabin is."

"Aimee can't go by herself."

"No, she can't," Matt agreed. "That's why I'm going. I'm pretty confident we can get up there in a vehicle. Trouble is, I think that winter storm may move in a lot earlier than predicted, so I'm not nearly so sure that we'll be able to get down, especially if the storm is a bad one. Do you think you could be on alert with your helicopter if we need you?"

"Yeah, sure. When are you going? Soon, I hope. You know my bird's not fond of snow."

"I know your bird will do whatever you tell her to."

"And you should hire yourself out to the local TV station as a weatherman. Hell, you're a hundred times better than those guys." It was an old joke.

"Hair gel and a blue screen? Sure. I'll do that the day you become a rodeo sharpshooter, firing at targets from under the neck of your horse." Matt couldn't help but smile. Then he got back to business. "The kidnapper told Aimee to be there at 1500 hours tomorrow. I just texted you the coordinates he gave us."

Deke opened the text and stepped over to an area map hanging on the wall. He traced the coordinates with his finger. "Here it is. It's pretty high up, and isolated."

"Yeah. I'm going to take one of our Hummers. There's a maintenance road up the south side. It'll take at least two hours to get up there."

"I see it. And I see what you mean. If the storm is bad, you won't be able to drive the Hummer back down."

"That's right. And we may have a baby."

Deke's brows shot up. "May? You don't think your kidnapper is going to turn over the kid?"

Matt grimaced. "That location gives me a bad

feeling. How's he going to handle a seven-month-old and make sure nobody gets the drop on him?"

"He'll have an accomplice."

"That plus the storm—I don't like the odds. That's why I need you to be available. I want to set up primary and secondary rendezvous points in case we can't use the Hummer to get out. Maybe even a tertiary." Matt paused and rubbed his neck. "The location he's picked is the worst place to be when that storm hits. He's got to know that. I have a feeling he's banking on it to cover his tracks."

He and Deke discussed locations, terrain, times and alternatives for a few minutes. Finally, Deke rubbed his eyes. "I think those look good."

"Me, too. If there are any major shifts in weather patterns, we can redo them."

"I'll have the bird ready to go," Deke said. "I know you know what you're doing, but be careful, riding out the storm up there. You two could be blown right off that mountain."

"Thanks for that image. Don't worry. I plan to be back down the mountain in the Hummer with Aimee and the baby, safe and sound well before Friday morning. That 0900 rendezvous is if we get caught by the storm or something goes wrong. If everything goes as planned, I'll be in touch, although we won't get back until after dark."

"Just make sure you've got plenty of flares."

"Don't worry. We'll have flares. Do the times work for you?"

"Times are fine. And I see you're planning to move up toward the peak, rather than down."

"Right. I figure if we can't ride back down in the Hummer, we need to be heading to higher ground. I'd like to try and stay either ahead of or above the storm. Plus, your bird's not going to like dodging trees, so the fewer the better."

Deke nodded.

"One last set of coordinates," Matt said, sending Deke a text. "These are for a last resort. A tertiary rendezvous. It's two miles south of the Vick's cabin."

Deke's phone pinged. "The hunting cabin. You think you might end up there?"

Matt shrugged. "It's good shelter. We might need it, if we have to travel that far."

"Sounds good. I'll be sitting on ready, waiting to hear from you."

"Thanks, man. I knew I could count on you." Matt stood.

"You know there's another way to handle this."

Matt frowned at Deke. "Not really."

"Sure there is. Leave Aimee out of it. You and I go up in the Hummer, get the drop on the kidnapper, and get the baby back safe and sound."

Matt sighed. "That would work, if one of us could pass for a medium-height, slender female.

But there's a bigger consideration. The baby. If everything goes well, which one of us is prepared to bring back a seven-month-old who needs his mother? Not to mention that nothing good comes from getting between a mother and her child. I'm not telling Aimee she has to stay behind."

AIMEE BURIED her nose more deeply into the high collar of her down parka. The Hummer was heated, but she was still cold. She'd rolled her balaclava up like a watch cap, ready to pull down over her face if she needed it, and she was beginning to think she needed it. The chill didn't come from the dropping temperatures outside, though. It came from her heart. As often as she told herself that William was safe, that the kidnapper couldn't afford to hurt him if he wanted his money, her heart remained unconvinced.

Matt's grim expression didn't help. He looked worried as he maneuvered the Hummer's steel snow tracks over the rough terrain. He glanced at her. "You okay?"

"Okay?" she croaked, then pressed her lips together. Control, she reminded herself. It's all about control. She had to hold herself together, for her baby's sake.

"If you're cold, there's a blanket under your seat."

She gave a harsh little laugh. "You think I'm worried about being cold?"

"Aimee, I know you're afraid something's going to happen to William. But I don't want you to neglect your own health. You're highly stressed, you're exhausted, and you could become hypothermic without even realizing it. I need to make sure you're warm and comfortable."

"I don't need to be comfortable. I don't want to be. I just want to get up there, get my baby back, and get home."

"That's what I want too," Matt said. "But part of my job is to take care of you."

She closed her burning eyes. *Control. Control.* She repeated it like a mantra.

"Damn it!"

She jumped and her eyes flew open. "What?"

"Sorry." His fingers tightened around the steering wheel. "I can't believe I let the kidnapper run the show. I should have demanded he do it my way. He would have. It's the money he wants. It's too dangerous for you up here."

"Where should I be? Back at home, all safe and warm? Waiting helplessly? No, thank you."

"Not helpless. Safe and warm. I don't like putting you in danger. Plus, with you here, I can't do everything I'd be able to do if I were alone."

"Sorry I'm cramping your style."

"That's not—" He stopped, and his jaw muscle worked. He kept his attention on the barely discernable path before them as the incline grew steeper, and the sky turned increasingly dark and gray.

Where they'd started out, near Sundance, spring was in the air, with new shoots of grass and fresh coverings of moss. As they'd climbed higher, the greenery turned brown, and patches of old snow dotted the ground.

Aimee hunched her shoulders in an effort not to shiver. Matt's hands were white-knuckled on the steering wheel. His face was expressionless, but his jaw was clamped tight. He looked like he had that fateful day. The day he'd brought her husband's body home. That memory spawned others. Like the argument she and Will had a few days prior.

"It's just a weekend, Aimee. A guys' trip. You're starting to sound a lot like my mother."

Aimee yelled back at him. "Well, for once, I agree with Margo. You have responsibilities here. Have you forgotten that I'm pregnant? That you're fighting cancer? You need to use your energy to get well. I need you to stay with me."

Will gathered her into his arms and kissed her. "I'll be with Matt. He's safe as houses. Safer. He never takes unnecessary chances."

He looked down at her and a tender solemnity came

over his face. "Don't ever forget, Aimee. I trust Matt as much as I trust myself. More, maybe. No matter what happens, you can count on him. Ask him anything. He'll do it."

Those last words had been prophetic. Will had asked Matt for something. Matt had obliged, and Will had died. The doctors had told them it could have been months before the lymphoma took Will. Long enough for him to know his child. But Will had stolen those last months from her and his son. And his best friend Matt had helped.

Then, when Aimee could have used a friend, Matt had disappeared for a year. Will had been wrong. She couldn't count on Matt.

"Aimee, tell me how it happened."

She started. "How what happened?"

"The kidnapping."

"Didn't Special Agent Schiff tell you?"

He nodded. "But I'd like to hear what you remember."

Aimee closed her eyes and folded her arms. "I've been over it in my head a hundred times. I should have heard him. I should have woken up." She shook her head. "How could I have slept while someone came into my house and stole my baby?"

"William wasn't in your room, was he?"

"No. My doctor suggested I try sleep training with him in a separate room. I shouldn't have listened to her. I should have kept him right beside me."

"Aimee, stop beating yourself up. You didn't do anything wrong."

"When did you realize he was gone?"

"The sun was in my eyes, and I knew I'd over-slept. William always wakes me up around 5:30 or so. He's such a sweet baby." She smiled. "He wakes up happy. I'll hear him through the monitor, cooing and laughing—" her voice broke and her throat closed up.

He shot her a glance. "The sun woke you?" he asked gently.

"It was almost 6:30. When I realized I hadn't heard him, I panicked. So many things can happen—"

"What did you do?"

"I grabbed the monitor. The camera points right at the head of the baby bed. But I couldn't see him. His crib looked empty." She took a shaky breath. "I ran across the hall. The door was open, and I always leave it closed. He wasn't there. He wasn't anywhere." She felt the panic rising in her chest, heard it in her voice, just like then. Had it only been yesterday morning? "So I called 911."

"Schiff said there was no sign of forced entry. You're sure it was a stranger?"

Aimee frowned at him. "What do you mean?"

He spread his hands in a shrug without taking

them off the wheel. "I just mean, is there anything specific you're thinking of when you say it was a stranger?"

She shook her head. "I just can't—it can't be anyone I know."

"Are you usually a sound sleeper?"

"No. Actually I've been having trouble." Aimee thought about the past seven months since William Matthew's birth. All the nights she'd lain awake, worrying that something would happen to him if she went to sleep. She'd slept and something had.

"What about the evening before?" Matt drove steadily, watching the road and glancing occasionally into the rearview mirror. "Did you drink anything? Take anything to help you sleep?"

"No," she answered indignantly. "I would never take a chance like that with William."

Matt nodded and drove in silence for a few minutes.

Thoughts and images chased each other helter-skelter through her brain. Had anything been different about that night? "I didn't do anything differently," she said finally, a little defensively. "My life revolves around William's, and his routine is pretty well set. I locked up the house and turned out the lights around nine, just like I always do. I bathed him at the same time as I do every night. We played the same games we always play, and then I put him to bed and went downstairs to the kitchen."

"So anyone who'd been watching the house could know almost to the minute what time you go to bed?"

Aimee nodded miserably. "Yes. My life is that ordinary. I make the same tea, use the same cup. Probably even the same spoon. I can't think of anything unusual—" she stopped. There had been one thing different.

"Aimee?"

"It's nothing. It has to be nothing." She was really twisted—or really desperate—to even be thinking what she was thinking.

"Tell me."

"This is awful. I can't believe I'm even saying it." She took a deep breath, preparing herself for Matt's ridicule. "The tea? It's a new blend. Margo bought it for me at the health food store. They told her it was good for insomnia."

Matt glanced at her, frowning.

"But Matt, I've been drinking it every night for almost a week now."

"Is it helping you sleep?"

"Yes," she said. She hadn't really thought about it, but she had slept better this past week than she had in a long time. "It is. You don't think—?" Her breath hitched. "No. Margo wouldn't. Not her own —her only grandchild—" She stopped, horrified at her thoughts. During the first moments after she'd realized William was missing, the thought had flitted through her brain, but she'd dismissed it. Margo was his grandmother. "No. She couldn't—could she?"

"You tell me," Matt said.

"But it's outrageous. Not even Margo—. I mean yes, she's been complaining about how hard it is for her to get anything done through the Vick Corporation board since Will died."

"What's that got to do with anything?"

"Will left everything to William, just like his dad left everything to him. Remember when Boss Vick died?"

"Sure, that summer after we graduated high school."

"Right. Will was all set to go into the Air Force, like you and Deke and Rook."

"Yeah. Then his dad died so he changed his mind and decided to go to the University of Wyoming."

"Right. To stay close to home. Margo convinced him that he had to run the business. Because when he turned twenty-one, the entire Vick Hotel fortune and responsibility fell into his lap."

"Will controlled everything."

Aimee nodded. "And Margo controlled Will," she said bitterly.

"And now?"

"Now that Will's dead, William stands to inherit all of it."

Matt looked at her questioningly. "What about until he's of age? Isn't Margo his trustee?"

"No. Will named me," Aimee breathed.

"So you vote the controlling interest. That must rankle Mrs. Vick."

"I go to the board meetings, but I've never opposed a single decision. Why would I?"

"But you could."

Aimee shrugged. "I suppose. You think she did it, don't you?

Matt glanced in the rearview mirror. "Think about it. What does she want? What does kidnapping her own grandson right from under his mother's nose accomplish?"

"Frightening me?" Aimee cast about for any possible explanation. "Making it look like I can't—"

"Like you can't take care of your own child. What would she gain if she had custody of William? She'd retain controlling interest in the corporation. But it's damned hard to get custody away from the mother. She'd have to prove you're unfit. That you couldn't protect your own child in your own home."

Aimee moaned under her breath. Hearing those words in Matt's carefully neutral voice made them sound ominously true.

"Sorry," he muttered. "But it would explain a lot."

Aimee's face felt numb. Her mind felt numb. Intellectually, she understood Matt's reasoning. If he was right, her mother-in-law was setting her up to take William away from her.

His words echoed in her brain, taunting her with their truth.

You couldn't protect your own child in your own home.

CHAPTER 3

Aimee was still reeling, still trying to process the idea that Margo could have kidnapped her baby, when she realized that Matt had tensed.

Nothing outwardly was different. His hands still held the steering wheel in a tight grip at ten and two. His expression was carefully neutral, if a bit tight. But tension suddenly crackled in the air, and it definitely came from him. He'd gone on alert.

"Matt, what's wrong?" she asked.

"Wrong?" He glanced in the rearview mirror.

"Don't act like you don't know what I'm talking about. Something's wrong. I can tell. Did you see something?"

He didn't reply.

His sudden transformation fascinated and frightened her. Yesterday, he'd been the consummate soldier on a mission. This morning he'd acted more like a protector. She was his charge, his responsibility. But now, in the blink of an eye, he'd morphed from protector to predator and he'd scented his prey.

She opened her mouth, but before she could speak, he turned sharply, veering off the stark mountain road and stopped. "What are you doing?" Fear raced through her.

"I'll be right back," he said. "If you hear or see anything while I'm gone, lie flat across the seat. The metal should protect you."

"Protect me? Matt—?"

"Do you understand?" He glared at her, his tone and the grim set of his face brooking no argument.

"Yes," she retorted.

He walked over to the edge of the graded area and stopped at the line of trees. For a couple of seconds, he surveyed the mountain road in both directions, then reached for his fly.

Aimee gaped. Was he—? He was! On the way to rescue her baby, he'd stopped to take a leak! She didn't know whether to scream or laugh. Was he that confident? Or that arrogant?

She reached for the door handle, prepared to jump out and yell at him for wasting time while her child was in the hands of strangers. But at that instant, he turned his head imperceptibly to his right, back the way they'd come. And she got it finally—his sudden transformation, his razor-sharp alertness. He'd detected a threat.

Her heart jumped into her throat and she twisted in her seat, looking behind them. But she didn't see anything. Of course, she wouldn't. Matt was former Air Force special forces. His skills and senses were sharper than an ordinary person's.

She watched as he took a step closer to the trees. The sight was awesome and frightening. The curve of his back and the set of his shoulders made her think of a leopard about to spring. Standing still, he might look like a regular guy, but when he moved—*oh my*.

All at once the very air around her went still. She hunched her shoulders, suddenly feeling fragile and human and alone. The nape of her neck prickled. Her pulse pounded in her ears. She didn't move, not even turning her head to glance at the spot where Matt had disappeared into the trees. She had no sense of how long she'd sat there, not daring to move, when she heard it. The crunch of twigs and rocks.

Someone was coming toward the Hummer from the opposite direction. Without hesitation, she threw herself down across the seats, avoiding the stick shift. It had to be Matt—didn't it? She squeezed her eyes shut as the footsteps came closer. Her fingers twitched. If only she had something she could use as a weapon.

The driver's side door opened. Panic exploded in her chest. She whirled in the seat and curled her fingers into claws.

"Aimee," Matt said. "Good job."

Relief washed over her. Her scalp tingled. She sat up and tried to hide her trembling nerves. "You sneaked up on me," she accused.

He slid into the driver's seat. "Sorry I scared you. I wanted to circle around, make sure we weren't being watched."

"I knew you saw someone. Why couldn't you have just told me? I'd have been a lot less scared." She blew out a breath between pursed lips. "Who was it? The kidnapper?"

He shook his head and started the engine. "Can't be sure," he said shortly.

He was lying. But she'd already figured out that he would tell her only what she needed to know, and then only when she needed to know it—in his opinion.

Once she had William in her arms and they were safe back at home, she'd let him know what she thought about his tactics. For now, as much as she hated to admit it, his air of command, his complete confidence, and even his predatory edge, made her feel safe and secure.

As the only child of older parents, she'd grown up with the weight of responsibility for them on her shoulders. She'd learned early that there was only one person she could count on. Herself. Then Will had died, leaving her pregnant and alone, and bowed by responsibility again. In the year since Will's death, maintaining control was the only thing that had kept her going.

Now, at the very time when it was more important than ever to stay strong for her baby's sake, she found herself tempted to relinquish her precious control to someone else—to Matt—and the urge frightened her. She lifted her chin. She was not going to depend on Matt. Her baby needed her to save him. She would.

After another fifteen minutes or so of navigating the winding mountain road, Matt pulled over again.

"What now?" Aimee looked in the passenger-side mirror. "Did you see something again?"

He shook his head. "We're five miles from the meeting point." He pointed to the GPS locator on the dashboard. "And twenty minutes from the meeting time. This is where I get out. I'll circle around, while you drive the rest of the way alone. You've got the baby seat, formula, diapers, and blankets. The GPS locator is programmed for the exact coordinates. It's a straight shot. Just stay on this road."

He pulled a folded sheet of paper from a pocket. "Here's a printout of the route in case something happens to the GPS. Now, let's go over everything one more time."

Aimee nodded shakily. "Please. I feel like I'm in some weird dream—like all of this is a nightmare and I'm going to wake up tomorrow morning holding William."

"With any luck, that's exactly what'll happen."

His words were kind, his voice gentle. Aimee had to clench her jaw to keep from crying. Time stretched out before her like an endless road. It would be hours before she'd be back home with William, safe and sound. Many hours and many opportunities for something to go wrong.

"Hey, Aimee," Matt said. He lifted a hand toward her cheek, then checked the movement. "It's going to be okay."

She lifted her chin. "Don't do that. Don't spout meaningless promises to me. I need to know what I'm up against. What if the kidnapper doesn't bring William? What if my baby's cold, or hungry—?" She bit her cheek. Control, she reminded herself. "What if he's as scared as I am?"

"Whoa. You can't worry about any of that. And remember, being scared is normal. You're very brave."

"Oh, yeah. I'm the bravest woman on the planet, driving up this remote mountain to rescue my baby from a kidnapper." Tears stung her eyes and a lump lodged in her throat. She was *so* not brave.

A tender look softened his sculpted features. "Listen to me. You are the bravest woman on the planet. And—" he paused for a second. "Will was the luckiest man in the universe. Aimee, I—"

"Don't." She stiffened, and held up her hands. "Please. Don't start. I have to think about William. I can't afford to get all emotional about what happened to Will."

Matt's expression closed down. He nodded. "Yeah. Best to hate me for one thing at a time," he said flatly.

She caught the sadness in his dark eyes before he averted his gaze. His words and the look surprised her. It wasn't like him to feel sorry for himself.

He shrugged it off and climbed out of the Hummer, pulling a daypack out with him. Then he leaned his forearms on the driver's side door. "I put on the emergency brake. Don't forget to release it before you head out."

She took a deep breath. "I've ridden ATVs in these hills all my life. I can handle this Hummer," she said.

He nodded matter-of-factly. "I've got my route planned out. Going straight up, it'll take me about fifteen to twenty minutes to reach the location the kidnapper gave us. If you drive no faster than fifteen miles per hour, we should arrive at about the same time since this maintenance road snakes back and forth and the terrain is getting rougher. Just stay on it. Don't get lost."

"I'll be fine."

"I know you will. But Aimee, I can't stress too strongly how dangerous this man could be. If anything—*anything*—goes wrong, you have to turn the Hummer around and head down the mountain as fast as you can. With or without William. Understand?"

"No. That is not happening. I'm not going anywhere without my baby."

"Listen to me. I have to know that you'll do what I say. I promise you, you won't have to deal with the kidnapper. I'm going to ambush him. I don't expect anything to go wrong, but if something does, I have to know you'll follow my orders. Do what I say. I can't do my job—I can't rescue William—if I have to worry about you. Your baby will be safe. I swear."

Aimee frowned, studying his face. There was something else—something he wasn't telling her. He wouldn't meet her gaze. Instead, he stared down at his clasped hands.

Suddenly she understood. "You don't think he's bringing William, do you?"

His head ducked lower for an instant. Then he straightened.

"Do you?" Aimee grabbed his hand before he could remove it from the car door. She held on until he bent down again. His dark eyes finally met hers—solemn, guarded.

"Oh—." Her heart cracked wide open, and all her careful efforts at control spilled out. She shook her head slowly, back and forth, back and forth. "No, please, Matt. Tell me my baby's okay."

He reached out and brushed a strand of hair from her cheek. "Aimee, I swear to God, if I have to die to make it happen, William will be back in your arms today, safe and sound."

THE KIDNAPPER WAS LIGHTER on his feet than Matt had expected, given his size and the bulky pack strapped to his back. His clothes and pack were a winter camouflage pattern that blended almost perfectly into the patchy snow and barren trees as he moved. And he moved well, silently as a woodland animal, alert to everything around him. An assault rifle, military-grade, was hooked over one shoulder.

Matt could tell he was former military. Maybe even former special forces. That explained this location, the timing, and the man's obvious comfort in his surroundings. Not many people knew how to glide silently through rough terrain, leaving almost no trail. Matt would bet money that this guy was also a survivalist. He had to have trekked every inch of this mountain, or he wouldn't have chosen it.

But was he here alone?

Matt had no doubt that he'd seen sunlight glinting off metal in the Hummer's rearview mirror as the vehicle had snaked back and forth up the maintenance road. That was why he'd stopped, to try and catch a glimpse of whoever was tailing them. But he hadn't spotted anything. Whoever had been back there was good. Probably as good as the man in front of him. Impressively close to Matt's own skills.

The question in Matt's mind was—were there two guys following him? This man could have followed them up the road and then cut through just like Matt had and beaten him to the ransom drop point. But it also was possible he had an accomplice, and the accomplice had followed them while this guy waited up here.

Matt couldn't afford to let down his guard, so until he proved otherwise, this man was the kidnapper, and in the vehicle following them was his accomplice.

Matt had to watch his back. He'd planned out as much as he could of his strategy. He too was dressed in winter camo and carried a small daypack. Besides binoculars, he was equipped with a compact MAC-10 machine pistol he didn't plan on using, a mini tranquilizer gun, and a few Flexicuffs.

His intent was to surprise the kidnapper and immobilize him with the tranq gun. Once he had him restrained, he could definitely make it worth the man's while to reveal the baby's location.

Matt crouched, hidden by scrubby bushes, and observed the kidnapper through his high-powered binoculars. The man was positioning himself for most cover and widest angle of sight.

For a couple of seconds, Matt held his breath, listening for the Hummer's engine, but he didn't hear anything. It was nerve-wracking, waiting up here, knowing Aimee was about to drive straight into the lion's den. All this would be so much easier if he didn't have to worry about her being hurt.

Matt shifted, examining the area around the kidnapper. He searched for signs of another person —someone whose job it was to take care of the baby. He used a careful mental grid layout he'd developed while he was in the Air Force.

The controlled search made it impossible to miss a person, much less a vehicle, but all Matt saw was a set of tracks made by a one-man snow-mobile. He saw nothing of the vehicle itself. The kidnapper had done a damn good job of hiding his vehicle and covering his tracks.

Matt's respect for him went up a notch, and his fear for Aimee's baby went up three. The suspicion that was planted in his brain from the first moment he'd seen the TV news still remained. It rooted itself more deeply, undermining his confidence.

If this man were simply a kidnapper out to make a quick million, and if he'd come to make a good-faith exchange, then why didn't he have the baby?

Matt continued his grid search until he'd covered every square inch of visible land surface. He saw nothing that indicated anyone but the kidnapper had been—or was—in the area. He pocketed the binoculars. *Damn.* He hated to be right about this one.

Although the kidnapper seemed to be all about money, and Aimee's revelations about Margo's need to control the Vick Corporation made her mother-in-law a prime suspect, Matt didn't believe it.

A silent vibration started near his left knee. His phone. Grimacing, he shifted enough to pull it out of the cargo pocket of his camo pants. Keeping one eye on the kidnapper, he glanced at the screen.

It was a text message from Deke. He focused on the letters. *Got passenger list—your flight. Hafiz Al Hamir, Afghan Natl. See photo.*

Matt cursed silently when he saw the photo. He'd seen that man before. He'd run into him several times in Mahjidastan. Still watching the kidnapper, Matt answered Deke.

Know Al Hamir. Trace him?

A sick certainty burned in his gut. Novus Ordo had engineered William's kidnapping to get his hands on Matt, to interrogate him about whether Rook was alive. That meant he wanted Matt alive. But Matt was sure Novus wouldn't blink at killing anyone who got in his way.

He'd known it. It had been a huge mistake to bring Aimee up here. He should have come alone, or brought Deke or another BHSAR specialist.

If he was right about Novus, and he was becoming more and more sure by the hour, she and her baby were disposable pawns in an international terrorist's effort to protect his identity.

The kidnapper was on the move again. Matt pocketed his phone and cleared his mind. He needed focus and hair-trigger response. If he failed to return William Matthew to his mother's arms, he'd have plenty of time for regrets and unbearable sorrow later. Right now, all he could concentrate on was his mission to get the drop on the kidnapper and rescue Aimee's baby. He didn't allow the thought that William wasn't here into his head. He had to operate as if he were.

He crouched in a position from which he could spring in a fraction of a second and let his senses feed him information. They were as clear as the mountain air. The smell of evergreen and the coming snow teased his nostrils. The tingling in his hands and face signaled the dropping temperature. And the quickly darkening sky telegraphed the approach of the winter storm—early, just as he'd predicted.

The only sound Matt heard was the rustling of bare tree branches and evergreen needles in the rising wind.

The kidnapper raised his head, as if sniffing a scent on the breeze. He appeared calm and relaxed, and yet poised to react with quick reflexes. Damn, the man was good.

A discordant hum rose in the distance. The Hummer. Aimee was almost here. The kidnapper swung the rifle from his shoulder and settled into a comfortable, balanced stance—observant and attentive—ready for anything.

Matt shifted, feeling the weight of the MAC-10 in its holster. He could get to it if necessary, but he didn't plan on using it. He held the tranq gun. The Flexicuffs were looped through his belt.

The Hummer's engine grew louder, its steady roar filling the air around them. The engine's noise blocked Matt's keen hearing, but it also covered any noise he might make when he sneaked up on the kidnapper.

After a glance around, Matt crept forward, until he was less than twenty yards away from the man. With his tactical-grade, compression-fit pants, he had far greater agility than the bulkily-dressed kidnapper. He could rush him, sink a tranq dart in his neck, and cuff him within seconds.

The Hummer crested the rise, and Matt's pulse kicked into high gear. He could barely make out Aimee's silhouette through the vehicle's tinted windows. As he watched, she slowed down, then rolled to a stop. *Stay in the vehicle. Make him come to you.* He silently recited the instructions he'd given her.

He'd retrofitted a loudspeaker for her to use for any necessary communications. He'd warned her not to exit the vehicle until the kidnapper produced the baby. And, as he'd reminded her not twenty minutes before, at the first sign of trouble, she was to turn the Hummer around and get out of there.

Those were her instructions. But Matt had other plans. He had no intention of letting the kidnapper within thirty yards of her.

She inched the Hummer closer. The kidnapper shifted to the balls of his feet, holding the rifle loosely yet competently, like a pro. Another point in his favor and more cause for concern on Matt's part.

Matt made his move. He rose from his crouch and crept around the edge of the clearing, keeping the scrub bushes between him and the other man. Once he got into position, it would take him less than thirty seconds to get behind him, slip out from the trees at the last second, then grab and tranquilize him. In a situation like this, thirty seconds was a hell of a long time.

He'd choreographed every step ahead of time. He'd had plenty of experience with stealth from rescue missions he'd conducted in the Air Force and afterwards while working for BHSAR. He knew how to approach an enemy and extract an innocent without detection. Given this guy's obvious expertise, he was glad to have the noise of the Hummer's engine as added cover.

He positioned himself directly behind the kidnapper. Staying low, he inched forward silently.

Then, without warning, something hit him from behind. With no more than a fifth of a second wasted on a startle response, Matt whirled. He rammed his fist and shoulder into his attacker's body. As his knuckles encountered flesh and bone, he followed through, putting his whole weight behind the blow. But it wasn't enough. His attacker was quicker.

Matt went down—hard.

The man grabbed a handful of Matt's hair and slammed his face into the frozen ground.

The blow dazed him. But the cold pressure of a gun barrel pressed to the side of his neck brought him back instantaneously. Adrenaline sheared his breath and cleared his brain. He jerked just as a quiet pop echoed in his ear. Something sharp scratched his neck. A pop. Not a bullet. It was a tranquilizer dart.

Damn! Even as the thoughts rushed through his brain, he torpedoed his elbow backwards. With a breathy grunt, the man fell away and his tranq gun went flying.

Before he hit the ground, Matt whirled and grabbed the other man's collar. With a renewed burst of energy, and using muscles he hadn't used in months, Matt heaved the man's bulk around, between himself and the kidnapper.

Pocketing his own tranquilizer gun, Matt slid the MAC-10 from its holster and buried its barrel into the flesh of his attacker's neck. He was tempted to rip off the man's ski mask, but to do that, he'd have to let go of the man or the gun.

"You nearly got me with your tranq dart, but believe me, this is not a tranq gun," he growled, scanning the area in front of him in case the kidnapper had heard them. "It's the real thing. And it will take your head clean off if you don't tell me who you are."

His answer was a blood-chilling string of curses, some English, some Arabic. Damn it, the kidnapper had to have heard.

"Are you Al Hamir?" he whispered.

The man's head jerked in surprise.

"So you are. Did Novus Ordo send you?" Matt dug the muzzle of the MAC-10 deeper into his flesh. His prisoner shook his head, but Matt saw the truth in the man's black eyes. "Tell me what you know about the kidnapping—"

The crack of exploding gunpowder hit his ears a fraction of a second before the bullet whistled past his head. He ducked.

Al Hamir used Matt's own elbow trick to knock the wind out of him, then leapfrogged across three or four feet of ground, diving for his own weapon. The kidnapper shot again.

Matt aimed the machine pistol at Al Hamir. But something was wrong. He couldn't clear his vision. He bent his head and squeezed his eyes shut for an instant. Just as he did, a second bullet grazed his ear.

He swallowed a pained cry and his hand flew to his ear. It came away bloody. His bloodstained fingers trembled as he stared at the proof of how close the bullet had come. If he hadn't paused to clear his vision, it would have split his skull.

A high-pitched scream, barely distinguishable above the roar of the Hummer's engine, sent his heart slamming into his chest. It was Aimee. She gunned the engine and the vehicle shot forward, toward the kidnapper.

Aimee, no! What was she doing? *Turn around. Get out of here.*

The kidnapper aimed at the Hummer's windshield.

At the same time, Matt saw Al Hamir whirl, brandishing a semiautomatic pistol.

Matt ducked down and rubbed his eyes. The scratch on his neck had absorbed some of the tranquilizer. Enough to blur his vision. He cursed silently and gave his head a quick shake.

The kidnapper yelled something that Matt didn't catch, then several bullets thunked into a tree to Matt's left. The kidnapper was shooting at Al Hamir again.

So, these two weren't working together.

Al Hamir yelped and toppled forward.

When Matt looked back at the kidnapper, the high-powered gun was aimed at his head. From that distance, the man couldn't miss. But before Matt could react and dive, the man swung his weapon back toward the Hummer.

Why hadn't he shot him? He might not get as good a chance again. Rising to a crouch, Matt took a precious split-second to make sure his head was as clear as possible, then sprinted toward the Hummer, spraying bullets on the ground in front of the kidnapper. He couldn't kill the man. He needed him alive—at least long enough to find out where William was being held.

As he crouched behind a stand of bushes, he heard the hitch in the engine noise that signaled shifting gears.

Yes, Aimee! Now turn around and get out of here!

But a Hummer didn't turn on a dime, or even a quarter. Still, she was trying. Careful to stay hidden, he lifted his head just in time to see the kidnapper raise his weapon and aim at the Hummer's windshield.

Alarm ripped through him. He was about to shoot Aimee. The high-powered blast would be enough to penetrate the tempered glass. Matt raised his weapon, his breath catching as his finger sought the hair trigger of the MAC-10.

Aimee would hate him if he shot the man who could lead them to her baby. But if he had to kill the kidnapper to save Aimee, then so be it. He'd find her baby some other way.

CHAPTER 4

Just as Matt's finger started to squeeze the trigger, the kidnapper lowered the barrel of his gun to the tires. Matt's scalp tingled with relief. At least he was no longer aiming at Aimee. Still, he had to stop him from disabling their only transportation down the mountain. He vaulted to his feet, brandishing the MAC.

"Hey!" he shouted. "You want your money? Then stop now! Or you'll never get it."

The tranquilizer he'd absorbed caused him to sway, but he caught himself. Blinking away the haze that tried to obscure his vision, he yelled, "You'll never see tomorrow!"

He strafed the ground in front of the kidnapper. But the other man didn't take the bait. His rifle barrel didn't even waver. He fired. A tire exploded with a loud crack. A second shot. A second crack.

The Hummer rocked dizzily, then tilted to the passenger side. It was going over.

Aimee!

Matt loosed another volley of bullets closer to the man's feet. He still hadn't ruled out killing him. The shooter dove for the ground, but immediately, he righted himself and fired again—this time at the Hummer's gas tank. Metallic thunks peppered the vehicle's frame.

Wincing at each shot, Matt tried to draw a bead on him, but the kidnapper's duck and roll had positioned the Hummer between them. Matt sprinted toward the vehicle. He had to stop him. It was only a matter of seconds before a bullet hit the tank.

The tranquilizer was doing more than turn Matt's world upside down, though. His legs were as heavy as lead weights. It was like a bad dream. He aimed the MAC at the kidnapper, but the Hummer with Aimee inside was still between them. Not only that, but he could smell gasoline. One of the man's shots had struck the gas tank.

Finally, Matt had a clean shot, but he didn't take it. Aimee was in the Hummer and the smell of gasoline was getting stronger. He had to get her out and away from the vehicle.

He started to run, pumping his legs as hard as he could. He'd be at the driver's door within two seconds. But the kidnapper was running too, and he was closer. Swallowing against the dizziness brought on by the tranquilizer, Matt pushed himself harder.

Aimee opened the driver's side door. "No!" Matt shouted, but she was already out. Then her foot slipped in the gasoline and she fell. When Matt looked back at the kidnapper, he saw him holding an old-fashioned silver cigarette lighter. He flipped open the lid.

Matt stopped and aimed, holding his breath and gritting his teeth as he kept the sights of the machine pistol steady.

The kidnapper's sharp gaze met Matt's as he dragged Aimee toward him and lifted her to shield him. As Matt watched helplessly, the kidnapper nodded at him, then struck the lighter and tossed it over Aimee's head and into the middle of the pool of gasoline.

The small flame looped through the air as if in slow motion. When it was a couple of inches above the puddle, the fumes caught and flared. By the time the lighter splashed into the liquid gasoline, the flames had leapt two feet into the air and were spreading.

The kidnapper jumped up and sprinted away.

Matt couldn't worry about him. The fire was growing, and flames were rising only inches from Aimee's legs.

"Aimee, get back!" he yelled.

She scrambled backwards, her eyes wide and bright with terror.

Pocketing his gun, Matt rushed toward her. A shot rang out—but not from the direction the kidnapper had run. It came from the south. Al Hamir. Matt dove the last few feet. He landed next to Aimee as red flames licked at her hiking boots.

Scooping his hands under her arms, he lifted her and heaved her as far as he could away from the flames and then dove on top of her, covering her body with his, shielding her head with his arms. Behind them, the flames roared and spit, like a massive beast. The ground trembled beneath them, and a whistling sound filled the air.

The flares! He'd packed a dozen into the rear of the Hummer.

"What's that?" Aimee whispered.

"It's okay," he whispered. "You're okay. Just stay still." Matt hunched his shoulders and pressed his cheek against hers, doing his best to shield every inch of her body with his. He could feel her panicked breaths against his cheek, hear them sawing in and out through her throat. He could smell the lemon sweetness of her hair. She stopped wriggling, and turned her head a little more, which put her lips about an inch away from his. He closed his eyes and pretended they weren't there.

He had no idea how many of the flares fired

because suddenly, with a deafening roar, the gasoline exploded. For an instant, the air grew totally still and quiet, as the conflagration sucked in oxygen. Then a blast of heat strafed them, like the breath of a fire-breathing dragon. Matt felt the sting of heat across the backs of his hands and the nape of his neck.

After several seconds, he lifted his head slightly and peeked at the Hummer. It was still engulfed in flames, but they were weakening.

Their supplies and equipment—everything—was burning up. He stiffened, and felt Aimee move beneath him.

"Matt?"

"Stay still," he commanded. He rose to a crouch with his weapon drawn and rapidly scanned the clearing, but they were alone. The kidnapper was gone.

He turned back to Aimee. "Why didn't you turn around and get out of here like I told you to?"

"He shot you!" she hissed. "I saw you go down. I thought you were dead. I had to save my baby."

He held her gaze for a moment, wanting to berate her for not obeying him, but she lifted her chin and stared at him with defiance in her eyes. It occurred to him that there was probably no emotion in humans stronger than the one radiating from her. The fierceness of the love of a woman for her child. There was no way he could counter that.

Setting the machine pistol down, he shrugged his daypack off his shoulders.

"What are you doing?" she asked.

Ignoring her, he quickly assessed his clothing. Had he landed in gasoline when he dove for Aimee? He didn't see any stains and didn't smell gas.

"Don't move," he said, pointing at the ground where she sat. "I'm going to see if I can salvage anything."

"You can't go near that," Aimee said. "Wait until the fire dies down."

He shook his head. By the time the flames died down, there would be nothing left. Hell, there was probably nothing left anyhow.

He approached the burning vehicle cautiously. Everything inside was black and smoldering, or still actively burning. By the red and yellow flickering light, he saw what was left of the baby car seat, melted down to a nearly unrecognizable lump of plastic. Behind it, in the back of the vehicle, he could see the damage caused by the flares that he'd packed in case they had to signal Deke in the dark. Then he spotted his backpack. There was nothing left of his supplies and equipment. The nylon webbing that crisscrossed its lightweight frame had burned and melted.

Matt cursed silently. Everything he'd packed so carefully, planning for any contingency, was burned and useless. His double sleeping bag, the concentrated nutrient packs, rain gear, snowshoes, spare batteries for the GPS locator and satellite phone, first aid kit, and even the water canteens were destroyed. He sucked in a deep breath and coughed as smoke scalded his throat. It was getting thicker and blacker as the flames died.

There was still plenty of heat, which would have come in handy if it weren't almost certainly toxic, judging by the smell. Between the upholstery, the gasoline, the oil and other fluids, and the various plastics and dyes, there was no telling how contaminated the air was.

They couldn't stay near that fire. He headed back to where Aimee was waiting. She took a breath to speak, but coughed when she got a lungful of smoke. She took his hand and let him help her stand.

She looked over her shoulder at the Hummer. "I need to get my bag. William's baby food and diapers and—"

"They're gone. Burned up. My supplies are too. We'll have to make do."

"But—"

"Come on. We need to get away from here. That smoke is toxic."

Aimee coughed again, proving his point. She looked up at him and gasped. "Oh! Matt, you're bleeding. It's all over your face and neck."

He touched his ear and winced, then looked at his hand. A fresh smear of blood stained his finger. "Don't worry. I'm okay," he said shortly, as a wave of dizziness reminded him just how handicapped he still was by the tranquilizer. "Hell, another quarter inch and the bullet would have missed me completely."

Aimee pushed his hand away and stood on tiptoe, looking at the wound. "That's not funny," she snapped as she touched the curve of his ear, near the raw scrape. "It looks like the bleeding has almost stopped."

He shrugged away her touch and picked up the MAC-10. "Stand behind me." He held the pistol waist-high and swept the clearing with it and his gaze.

She grasped his sleeve and pointed toward the east. "He ran into the woods in that direction. We've got to go after him."

Matt twisted away from her grip and put a hand on her shoulder. "He's long gone. The fire gave him a big head start."

"No! We've got to go. We have to catch up."

"Aimee. He's twenty minutes ahead. It's getting dark. We'll never catch up to him tonight."

She turned and stared at him, the brightness of her green eyes fading as understanding dawned. Her hands covered her mouth. A flake of snow caught on her lashes.

"But he's still got William!" she cried.

A giant fist squeezed his heart at the utter desolation on her face and in her voice. He opened his mouth to lie, to feed her false hope. "We'll find him, Aimee. Don't worry."

"Don't worry? Don't—?" She gulped in a desperate breath. "He's my baby. He's so little. He's only seven months old. He will die without me. Don't tell me not to worry!"

He steeled himself for her attack, figuring she had a perfect right. He hadn't kept his word. He'd let both men get the best of him. One had sneaked up on him because he'd let his guard down. The other had turned his own equipment into a weapon against him.

But she didn't attack him. She pressed her fists to her eyes. "What do we do now?" she whispered. "We don't have my baby, and he doesn't have his money."

Matt gently pulled her hands away from her face. Then he touched her chin. "Aimee. Look at me."

She raised her gaze to his, and he winced at the unbearable sorrow in her eyes.

"The money won't be transferred until we have William Matthew."

"The money won't be transferred?"

Matt nodded. "Not until we have William Matthew."

"So he has to take care of my baby."

If the money is what he's after. Matt didn't say anything.

For an instant, he allowed himself to bask in the joy on her face. Then a flake of snow drifted past her cheek, followed by another, and another. He looked toward the west. The sky was dark with thick gray clouds. He grimaced and shivered as a fat snowflake slipped down the back of his neck.

"We'd better get going," he said. "The storm's heading this way. As soon as it's over, I'll call Deke and we'll—" He bent over to pick up the daypack and suddenly the world turned upside down. His knee hit the hard ground with a painful thud.

"Matt?"

He jerked his head up. Her blurry, wavering face filled his vision.

"Matt! What's wrong?"

"I'm okay. I got a little dose of a tranquilizer dart when the second guy grabbed me. It's almost worn off."

"Tranquilizer dart?" Aimee's smile faded. "I don't understand. Why did the kidnappers need a tranquilizer dart?"

He rubbed his eyes and shook his head, trying to dismiss the question. But she wouldn't let it go.

"Matt? These men—why bring all those weapons—" she stopped, her eyes narrowing. "Why did you bring a machine gun?"

He met her gaze, his throat spasmed, and the punishing fist tightened and twisted in his chest until his heart wanted to burst. But before he could answer, she lifted her chin.

"Okay. Let me make it easier on you. Just answer this one question for me. The question you never answered yesterday. How did you happen to show up back in Wyoming just in time to be available when William was kidnapped?" she asked.

"What?"

"You—heard—me." A muscle ticked in her jaw and her nostrils flared. She took a step toward him, holding his gaze. "I woke up at six-thirty yesterday morning to find that my baby had been abducted from right under my nose. And then before noon, you showed up." She pressed her fingertips to her mouth for a second. "You might have been here for days, or weeks, for all I know."

Matt swallowed. "I flew in Tuesday night."

She nodded shakily. "Not even two days." She looked away, as if composing herself, and then looked at him again. "Why?"

"Why what?"

"Matt, stop it. Why did you fly back here on Tuesday, and my baby was kidnapped on Wednesday? Am I supposed to believe that was a coincidence?"

"Aimee, I don't know what you're thinking—"

He was lying again. He knew exactly what she was thinking. *What was the connection?*

"Answer me."

More snowflakes fell. The storm was almost upon them. By sheer force of will he stopped himself from examining the sky. Aimee needed as much assurance as he could give her right now, which admittedly wasn't much.

"I came back to Wyoming because Irina called me back. She had to stop looking for Rook."

Aimee's mouth fell open. "Had to stop? Oh, no. I didn't think she would ever give up. She must be devastated."

He nodded. "She is. But she can't do it anymore. She's out of money."

A little frown appeared between her brows. "She called you last week?"

He nodded, wondering what she was thinking. She didn't have the information he and Deke had. She knew nothing about Rook's relationship with Novus Ordo, or the threat Rook had posed to the mysterious terrorist as long as he was alive.

"These men—"

"Aimee, I don't know either of them."

She shook her head slowly. "This isn't about my baby at all, is it?" Her hands pressed against her chest, as if trying to stop the pain. "Oh," she gasped. "That other man. He wasn't speaking English."

"I don't know them—" he repeated, but she cut him off with a gesture.

"But you know who they are, don't you?" she snapped. "They have something to do with whatever you've been doing overseas. They followed you back here to Wyoming. Somehow, they knew they could get to you by kidnapping my baby."

"Aimee, don't think about—"

"They don't care about William. They want you," she whispered. "For all you know, my baby is dead."

CHAPTER 5

MATT CAUGHT Aimee's shoulders as she swayed. "Listen to me," he said firmly.

She steadied herself by closing her fingers around the sleeves of his sweater.

"William is still alive. I know he is." Dear God, he hoped she believed him. The doubt in his voice was clearly obvious to him.

She looked at him, her eyes filled with doubt and despair. Slowly, a little of the anguish faded from her expression. "Do you really think so?"

He forced his stiff lips to smile. "I know so. I swear, Aimee, I have no idea who these men are, but they are not going to let anything happen to William. They want that money." He hoped his desperate explanation sounded reasonable.

He took a deep breath. "And now we've seen them. We can identify them. Whichever one has

William, he can't afford to let anything happen to him now." He did his best not to wince. He wasn't sure if it was the tranquilizer circulating in his blood, or the desperation clouding his brain, but his reasoning had holes so big he could have driven the Hummer through them.

He prayed that Aimee wasn't thinking rationally enough to dispute him. Right now, what she needed was reassurance, not raw truth. And she certainly didn't need to know that he echoed her suspicions. He wasn't sure who either of the men was, but he knew there was more going on than just the kidnapping of a baby for money.

He shook his head, trying to shake off the tranquilizer's effect, and another snowflake slid inside the neck of his sweater. He looked up at the sky. Within an hour, the sun would go down, and then the mercury would plummet. They were fast running out of time.

He had to make a decision. Several, if he could remember what they were. A lungful of icy air helped to clear his head. He glanced at his watch and then stared at the tangle of briar bushes where he'd last seen the terrorist who'd followed him from Mahjidastan. He had to check on him.

He knew the man was wounded. He'd heard him shriek when the kidnapper's bullet had hit him. But after that, the terrorist had fired a shot. Had that been a last brave effort of a dying man?

Or a parting shot before he escaped to lick his wound? He had to find out. Matt rubbed his temples. At least he finally had made a decision.

"Aimee, get over here and stay behind me. I need to check the briar bushes over there, where Al Hamir fell. He could still be there."

"Al Hamir?" Her eyes widened, then immediately narrowed. "You know his name? I thought you said you didn't know either of them."

He sighed and spread his hands. "I don't. I got a text message from Deke, telling me—" He stopped. "It's complicated, Aimee. I just need you to trust me."

She shook her head slowly. "Do I have any choice?"

"No," he said grimly. "Have you shot a pistol before?"

"No. Rifles, shotguns, bows. But not a pistol." She sounded like she was about to cry.

"It's okay," he said, pulling the small handgun from his daypack. "This is a Glock." He handed it to her. "It's loaded, and it doesn't have a safety, so it's ready to shoot. You pull the trigger the same way you do a rifle. And you hold it in both hands, like the cops on TV. Okay?"

"I think so," she said.

He took her right hand and wrapped it around the gun, placing her index finger flat along the edge of the trigger guard, then he wrapped her left hand around her right. "Your left hand is there to steady your right. Got it?"

She nodded.

"Trust me, Aimee, you probably won't have to use it. But I need to know. Can you shoot a man if you have to?"

She lifted her chin. "Will it help me get William back? Then yes I can."

"Okay. Stay directly behind me. By now the guy's either dead or long gone. But there's no way I'm leaving the area until I verify that he's not waiting to ambush us."

Aimee met his gaze. "I'm ready."

The determination in her expression told him she meant it. To his surprise, something welled up in his chest until it almost cut off his breath. Her bravery and trust awed and scared him. "Good," he said roughly. "Let's go."

He held the MAC-10 at waist level, ready to shoot if necessary, as he moved cautiously toward the bushes. A couple of feet away, he held up his hand. "Wait here. Remember what I told you in the car? Same goes here. If you hear anything—anything at all—hit the dirt. Copy?"

"Yes."

He crouched and crept forward to the edge of the patch. Peering through the tangle of briar-studded vines didn't work. They were too thick. He straightened carefully, mindful of the lingering effects of the tranquilizer, but it seemed to finally be wearing off. So, with his weapon at the ready, he moved close enough to see over the top of the vines.

The briars covered about four feet of ground. Beyond that, he saw new scrapes and crushed twigs and leaves.

Glancing back at Aimee, he drew a circle in the air with his left hand. "I'm circling around," he mouthed, then held up his palm. "You stay there."

She nodded carefully.

He circled around and bent to study the scrapes on the ground. In amongst the dried leaves and twigs, Matt saw a saucer-sized pool of blood. Beyond it, dark red drops drew a path toward the trees, like shiny red bread crumbs left by Hansel and Gretel. *Wounded, but not fatally.*

He followed the trail of blood toward the trees, dividing his attention between the ground and the wooded area ahead of him.

At the edge of the clearing, he stopped. For a few seconds, he stood still, listening for the sound of a motor, but all he heard was the wind rustling the bare branches. Carefully, he followed the blood trail for a few more steps, until the underbrush was too thick to penetrate and the tree's roots met and intertwined on the ground.

He backed away, staying in his own footsteps.

Before he reached the stand of bushes, he felt Aimee behind him. He turned.

"When I tell you to stay put, I mean it," he said sternly, wishing he felt like smiling at her obstinate expression. Her legs were shoulder-width apart and she held the Glock like every cop on Law & Order, although her expression better resembled a terrified witness.

"The kidnapper definitely wounded him. He's losing a good bit of blood. I don't think he'll try anything else. If he's got any sense, and if he's got a vehicle—which I'm sure he does—he's probably headed down the mountain by now."

"What do we do now?" she asked.

He frowned. "If I had the Hummer, I'd send you down in it. But without it, we're not going anywhere, except to find a way to get you out of this storm." She shivered and hunched her shoulders against the wind. She was already feeling the cold, even in her down parka and balaclava.

His base layer was keeping him warm so far. If he thought it would help her, he'd strip it off and give it to her. But the suit had been custom-fitted to his body for maximum insulation. It would be much too large for her, and therefore useless. Besides, if he was going to keep her safe, he had to keep himself warm and mobile.

Aimee still held the Glock. He pulled his parka from his daypack and shook it out to fluff the down before putting it on. Then he lifted the daypack onto his shoulders and stowed the Glock in a side pocket.

After glancing up at the sky one more time, he pulled the satellite phone out of his pocket and looked at it. No signal. Why was he not surprised? He wasn't sure if the problem was the cloud cover or the cold, but it didn't matter. There would be no nighttime rescue tonight. He couldn't contact Deke or anyone else until the storm passed.

He put the phone away and retrieved the GPS locator. Again, no satellite reception. He'd have to rely on old-fashioned methods of finding his way. He'd memorized the maps so he knew where they were going. He just hoped they could make it before the storm caught up to them in full force.

It was almost 1900 hours. Seven o'clock. They had—at best—thirty minutes of daylight left. A stab of apprehension pierced his chest. He'd mapped three shelters within reasonable distance of the ransom drop point. The one closest to his primary rendezvous point was 4.8 miles, heading 41 degrees, almost directly east. The next closest to rendezvous was 4.5 miles at eighteen degrees.

The third shelter would be the easiest walk. It was two miles away, and the route was relatively flat. However, the direction was 30 degrees, which put it farthest from the primary rendezvous point.

He could picture the grid in his head. If he were

alone, he'd head directly for the closest shelter. 4.8 miles would be less than an hour at his usual pace, even in snow.

But he figured Aimee could cover about three miles per hour at best, and that didn't take the storm into consideration. It would take her almost two hours. Which wouldn't be so much of a problem if they'd gotten started an hour earlier.

But they hadn't. And as he'd feared, the storm was moving in at least three hours ahead of predictions, just like he'd told Special Agent Schiff. He had no choice but to head for the nearest shelter, even if it was farthest from the primary rendezvous point.

"How far do we have to go?" Aimee asked, as if she were reading his mind.

"With any luck, we can make it in an hour or a little more," he said, knowing he was being optimistic. The longer it took, the harder it would be. He could smell the snow in the air, and he figured the wind was already up to twelve miles per hour. His prediction was that it would reach fifty miles per hour or more before the storm played out. And Matt didn't want to be caught out in it.

He sure as hell didn't want Aimee exposed to those temperatures and wind speeds. Not to mention that snow would lower visibility. Once they made it to the shelter, they could get a good night's sleep and get an early start.

Plus, as soon as the storm moved out, he could contact Deke and arrange a new, closer rendezvous point. He could tell Deke to bring replacement gear and supplies and pick up Aimee.

He shook his head. Getting Aimee to leave without her baby was going to be a trick. Surely two former special forces soldiers could convince one small civilian female to get into a helicopter. Yeah, right.

"We'd better get going," he said gruffly.

She looked up at him and a couple of snowflakes caught in her lashes. They looked like stars sparkling in her eyes. She blinked and scrunched up her nose, and desire lanced through his groin, surprising the hell out of him. *Damn*. At least it chased the drowsy haze from his head.

AIMEE FLEXED her right shoulder and suppressed a groan. It was already sore, and she had a feeling it would be black and blue by morning. She'd landed on it when the kidnapper had tossed her aside.

Matt glanced up as if he'd heard her. When she met his gaze, he gave her a little nod and then quickly looked back down at the small electronic device he held.

His effort to be reassuring wasn't very successful though, mostly because he wasn't the kind of guy who could hide his feelings. Throughout high school, college, and her marriage, Will and his three closest friends had been inseparable. They'd called themselves the Black Hills Brotherhood because of the near-death experience they'd shared as kids.

She knew all of them, but she knew Matt the best because he'd been Will's best friend. It was interesting how alike the four were—and how different. Deke Cunningham and Rook Castle would have had no trouble winning at poker. Even Will had always had a pretty good poker face.

Matt, on the other hand, was as easy to read as a first-grade storybook. Like right now. His brows drew down in a vee across his forehead as he looked at the tiny black screen of his device and then up at the cloudy sky. He was worried about them reaching shelter before the storm hit. She was worried, too. It was getting dark, and the wind was picking up.

She wasn't sure why she'd asked about going back down the mountain. Maybe because it would have been nice to have a choice, even though she'd never leave without her child. Or maybe so she could understand exactly how bad things were, now that the Hummer had been destroyed. They were on their own, with no transportation, a snowstorm on its way, and not one but two men who wanted to harm them. And her baby was still missing.

She figured she had a pretty good handle on how bad things were. Following Matt's instructions, she'd dressed for the trip as if they were going to picnic at the North Pole. Layers, layers, and more layers, he'd told her. Of course, she'd lived in Wyoming all her life, so she knew how quickly the weather could change in the mountains, especially this time of the year. She knew that the most important thing to remember was to keep one's body core warm, so she had put on a tank top, a base layer on top and bottom, a cotton pullover, a polyester sweater, and her down parka. She had dressed for any temperature.

She looked over at Matt, who was still studying the weather. "Is everything okay?" she asked.

He stuck the device into a pocket of the small daypack he carried on his back and then smiled at her. "Sure. We need to get a move on, though. Like I told you, it's going to take us an hour or so to get to the nearest shelter. And that storm is catching up to us."

She clenched her fists inside her gloves and bit her cheek in an effort to stop the tears that stung her eyelids. "Remind me again how everything is going to be all right?" she begged.

Matt tugged off his glove with his teeth and took it in his other hand. He stepped closer to her and touched her cheek, then her chin, with his warm fingers. "Hey," he said, coaxing her chin upward so he could look into her eyes. "Your cheeks are cold. Roll down your balaclava. It's going to get colder fast, once the sun goes down, which will be in about a half hour."

"I'm a little chilly," she admitted. "Matt? How sure are you that William is okay?"

A shadow of doubt flickered across his face as he curled his lips in a smile. "Very sure. I promise you, we'll find him and he'll be fine."

As he spoke, the weight of worry that was squeezing her chest let up a little. It occurred to her that whatever he told her, she believed it without reservation. It was strange that his thoughtful answer, coupled with the uncertainty that had briefly touched his features, made him more believable than her husband, Will, who had often stared at her expressionlessly rather than give her a straight answer. She watched Matt closely. Was he more trustworthy than her husband had been? Or was Matt, too, protecting her from the truth?

His teeth scraped lightly across his lower lip as he checked his pack and got ready to go.

Aimee arched her shoulder again. He'd said it would take about an hour to get to the shelter. She hoped he was being realistic, although she was afraid he was overestimating how fast she could move.

As they walked, Matt kept glancing at her. She kept her head high and trudged along, doing her best to keep up with him. "You still cold?" he asked.

"Oh, I'm fine." She shrugged.

He chuckled. "It's thirty-five degrees. You've got a right to be chilly. I told you to pull your cap down." He reached toward her balaclava.

"I'll do it," she said, pushing his hands away and pulling the balaclava over her face.

"Okay, good. What I told you before is still true. When I tell you something, I need you to do it." He pointed to the east. "This way."

"Where exactly are we going?"

"We're heading for a shelter for tonight. Then tomorrow Deke will pick us up."

"But we don't have William yet." Matt sent her a quick sidelong glance, and she realized that she had sounded faintly hysterical.

"We will. I promise, Aimee. We will."

She nodded, although she was no longer sure he was telling her the truth. "I know," she murmured. "I know."

FOR THE NEXT half hour or so, Aimee kept up with Matt better than he would have expected. Not so much better that he revised his estimate of how long it would take them to get to the shelter, but fast enough to keep his body producing heat, and from the sound of Aimee's breathing, she was keeping her heart rate up, too.

That was the good news. The bad news was that the storm was about to catch up to them. The wind was eastward, so it helped propel them forward, but the sun had gone down, the sky was cloudy and dark, and the air was heavy with moisture, making the wind bitingly cold.

They didn't talk much, just trudged along doggedly. Most of their conversation consisted of Matt asking if she was all right and she replying that she was. Then it started to snow, and Aimee started slowing down—way down.

He figured they were at least another half hour from the shelter. The temperature had dropped by another ten degrees, he was sure, and the wind was probably up to thirty miles per hour, enough to make Aimee stumble and him have to tense against it. He wrapped an arm around her waist and half-supported her, pushing her to walk a little faster. "Come on, Aimee. We're getting close. You've got to keep moving, or you're going to get sick."

"I am cold," she admitted for the first time. Her words sounded slurred. He reached back to a pocket of his daypack and retrieved a windup flashlight. He gave it about a minute of winding. Then he shined it in her face.

"Wha—?" she said, her hand coming up to block the light.

"Stop for a second," he said. "I just want to take a look at your face."

"No. I'm fine." She kept going, one foot in front of the other, shuffling along. "I wanna get there."

"Aimee," he said more loudly. "Stop." He gripped her arm. She tried to pull away from his grasp, but it was a half-hearted effort.

"No. Keep going," she muttered.

He shined the flashlight on her face again and saw how translucent and gray her lips looked. He aimed the light at her eyes. How did the prettiest, plumpest snowflakes always catch in her lashes? They drifted away as she blinked against the flashlight's bright beam. Her pupils were dilated and barely reacted to the light.

Fear arrowed through him. She was hypothermic. If they didn't get to the shelter soon, she could die.

CHAPTER 6

MATT KNEW hypothermia didn't require freezing temperatures to affect someone. But he also knew they were being pummeled by winds that made the temperature, which was already below freezing, seem at least five degrees colder. Plus the snow was wet, and dampness was seeping into their clothing.

He pulled off his down jacket and wrapped it around Aimee and snapped it closed. That gave her two layers of down, the best light insulation there was. Then he dug the hood out of its pocket and tugged it down over her balaclava. He should have done that a long time ago, but he'd overestimated her endurance.

"Not a good idea," she muttered.

"What?"

"Now you'll be cold. We'll both be cold." She giggled faintly.

He was worried about her. "Come on, Aimee, we're not far from the shelter. Let's race."

"No," she drawled. "Don't wanna race. Tired."

"I know," he said, putting his arm around her again to support her and urge her on ahead.

"Sleepy, too. I need to get home. William's waiting for me."

"Aimee, do you know where we're going?"

For a moment, she didn't answer. Then quietly, almost too quietly for him to hear, she spoke. "Home?"

He tightened his arm around her waist. "Listen, Aimee. We're up on Ragged Top Mountain. We're having an adventure. It's kind of like a treasure hunt." The wet snow was beginning to penetrate his wool sweater and underwear. He shivered, wishing he had the waterproof poncho that had burned up in his backpack.

"It's really important that we get to the shelter within the next twenty minutes. Can you walk really fast?"

She nodded. "I'm not sure. My feet aren't there." She laughed, a sound like ice cubes tinkling in a glass. "I mean, they're there. I just can't feel 'em."

"That's okay. They're there. I can see them." Matt smiled at her and looked up at the dark, cloud-filled sky. *God, help me get her to the shelter in time. Don't let me lose her. William needs her—I need her.*

MATT LIFTED the blankets that hung over the door to the shelter and pushed Aimee inside.

He'd already made her wait while he reconnoitered to be sure no one else was there. He figured both the kidnapper and Al Hamir already had a destination. The kidnapper was headed for wherever he was keeping the baby. And if Al Hamir had any sense, he'd get off the mountain and attend to his wound.

The shelter was primitive, with three walls and a wide opening on the east side. Blankets were the only coverings for the two windows that faced north and south. The inside was ice-cold, but the shelter's version of ice-cold was at least ten degrees warmer than the outside. He shuddered as his body took note of the small increase in warmth.

After shrugging off the daypack, he shined the flashlight's beam around. Two cots, a fireplace, a couple of chairs. He examined every inch of the space.

Firewood? Where was firewood? Then he saw it. A small pile of limbs and branches against the far wall. Under a window. Coated with a sheen of snow. What idiot had stored the firewood there? He grimaced. The wood was wet.

"Matt?" Aimee's voice quivered.

He pulled her toward one of the cots. "I've got

to get you out of those wet clothes and under the covers. Hurry."

She looked at him without moving.

He pushed his jacket off her shoulders and jerked the insulated hood and balaclava off her head. Her hair was wet and she was shivering so much her teeth chattered.

"Okay, Aimee. We're going to get you warm. Trust me?"

"I'm a little chilly," she whispered.

"I know, sweetie, I know." He unzipped her down parka and pushed it down her arms. "I'm just going to get these wet things off of you, okay?"

She nodded shakily. "I'm sleepy."

"That's good," he lied. His second lie to her.Drowsiness was a symptom of hypothermia, a severe one. It meant her body temperature was dropping to dangerous levels. He had to work fast.

By the time he got the parka and her hiking boots off, she'd almost quit shivering. That wasn't a good sign, either.

He talked to her while he undressed her. Nonsense things. Little reassurances, endearments, like one might use to soothe a frightened child. Finally, she was down to a little tank top and panties. They weren't wet, but there wasn't enough to them to provide any warmth. All they were good for was preserving a little of her modesty and titillating him a little.

Her skin was cool to the touch, and her fingers and toes were cold. He examined them closely, but they didn't appear to be frostbitten—yet. He was tempted to rub them, but he knew better. Too much rubbing could damage freezing skin and nerves permanently.

He checked out the cots, which, thank God, weren't near the windows. The blanket he unfolded was slightly damp, but it was made of wool. Even wet, wool would still keep her warm—once he got her warm.

He lay her down on the cot and put the blanket over her.

"Stay there, okay? I need to get a fire going." He grabbed two blankets from the other cot and piled them over her, too.

Then he turned to the fireplace. The wood stacked inside it was wet, like all the other firewood. He brushed the snow away from the wood piled under the window and dug through it.

Toward the bottom, he found some sticks that weren't wet through. Grabbing an armful, he stacked them in the fireplace and took a couple of wet weather, fire starter sticks out of his daypack. He placed them under the branches and lit them with all-weather matches.

The starter sticks flared immediately. Now if the wood would catch before they burned out. He adjusted a limb here, a branch there, until he was sure it was arranged for the best draft, and that was it. That was all he could do. He watched for a few seconds, encouraged by the crackling and spitting as the hot flames generated by the starter sticks burned off the dampness.

Once he was as sure as he could be that the wood was catching fire, he stripped down quickly, until he was covered in nothing but his boxer briefs and goosebumps. All his clothes were wet, even the insulated underwear. He was shivering, and he knew his body temp was down, but he wasn't hypothermic, thank God. His core was still warm.

Working as quickly as he could, and keeping one eye on the struggling fire and one on Aimee, he spread their clothes on chairs that he sat in front of the fireplace. If he could keep the fire going, maybe they'd dry by morning. He found a few hurricane candles on a shelf and lit them, then carefully poked at the fire, checking the draft. To his relief, some of the small branches were burning well.

"Hey Aimee, I think we're going to have a fire before too long." He rose and picked up one of the hurricane candles. Crossing the room to the cot, he held it so the light shined on her face.

"Aimee, are you awake?" Her eyes were closed and she was lying too still. He touched her cheek, then reached under the blanket and found her hand. Icy. Damn it. He looked at her fingers. They were still white and pinched.

"Okay," he said, hoping his voice sounded calmer than he felt. "I tell you what we're going to do. I'm going to move the other cot next to the fire and lay you there. I've got a mummy bag—that's a head-to-toe sleeping bag, made for subzero conditions. It's a single, but if I unzip it, we can both get under it, like a blanket. How does that sound?"

He didn't like that she was unresponsive. He knew how to treat hypothermia, but most recommended treatments assumed that dry clothes and a heat source were available. Until the fire grew enough to actually generate heat, Matt only had one source of warmth available—his own body.

He checked the other cot. At least it was no wetter than the one Aimee was on. He pulled it over in front of the hearth, grabbed two of the blankets from on top of Aimee, and spread them over the mattress. The wool would hold the heat in.

Then he bent over Aimee. "Aimee, sweetie, can you wake up? I need you to wake up for me."

She stirred and opened her eyes. They were glassy and not quite focused. "Is it William?" she whispered.

His heart twisted. She was dreaming, maybe even hallucinating. "Aimee, listen to me. Sit up for me. Can you tell me how you feel?"

"I'm tired," she said. "Sleepy."

"I know. And you can go to sleep, just as soon as

we get you over closer to the fire and get you warm. Come on. Let's move over to the fireplace."

She pushed at the blankets covering her.

"That's good. Here. I'm going to pull the covers down so you can get up."

Her eyes met his briefly. "Matt," she said. "What a nice surprise. Will's going to be so glad you're here."

He'd thought he couldn't carry any more guilt, but her slurred words cut him to his soul. She was hallucinating. She thought Will was still alive, thought they were all still friends.

No worries. Tomorrow she'd remember and hate him again. *If she lived until tomorrow.* Unless he got her warm, she wouldn't last that long.

"Let's go," he said and lifted her to her feet. She almost collapsed against him. He wrapped his arm around her waist and half-carried her to the cot.

Her skin felt cold, pressed against his. He had to get her body temp up and fast. "Here we are," he said softly. "Just lie down there, and I'll get the sleeping bag."

She obeyed him without protest. She lay down and closed her eyes. "Cold," she murmured.

"I know, Aimee, but I'm going to fix that." He grabbed his daypack and retrieved the small bundle that was the compressed down sleeping bag. He pulled it out of its stuff sack, unzipped it, and shook it out to fluff the down. "I'm just going to lay the sleeping bag over you, and then I'll put a couple of blankets on top."

He looked down at her. She lay on her side, facing the hearth, with her arms wrapped around her middle. The warm light from the fire made her pale skin look the color of a ripe peach. Her bare legs and arms were silky and delicately muscled. The little top and panties emphasized her slender curves. Her dark hair was still damp and beginning to wave around her face. She looked like she had in high school. Fresh, beautiful, vibrant. No wonder Will had fallen in love with her. Matt swallowed against the lump that rose in his throat from just looking at her.

He fetched two more blankets. The down inside the sleeping bag was the ideal insulator. It was lightweight and held in heat and wicked out moisture. But Matt wanted some weight on top to seal in the heat his body produced because he couldn't afford to waste even a couple of calories to the chilly room.

He carefully placed the blankets over the spread-out sleeping bag. Then, after a check of the fire to be sure it was lit and growing, he slid under the covers. Aimee's back was to him, so he cautiously moved closer. The scent of lemon assaulted his nostrils. How, after everything she'd been through, did she still smell so fresh and clean?

Her skin was cold, but apparently his body

didn't care. When his groin came in contact with her backside, he swallowed a moan and grimaced. The feel of her supple body affected him—a lot. He felt himself growing hard, felt his heart rate rise. Clenching his teeth and cursing himself for his weakness, he pulled away.

Aimee whimpered and scooted backwards slightly.

Since her skin felt cool to him, his must feel hot to hers. "Okay, Aimee. I'm going to get as close to you as I can—" *and keep my sanity.* "It's just to warm you up. I promise I won't make you uncomfortable." Too bad he couldn't promise himself the same thing.

He scooted closer, wrapping his arm across her shoulders and pulling her close to his chest. He knew he had to concentrate on her core, rather than her chilled arms and legs. What made hypothermia deadly was that the body got chilled through. The most important thing was to warm up the vital organs. Once her core temperature rose, her arms and legs would start warming up. He gritted his teeth and pressed his thighs against the backs of her legs.

Keep it professional, Parker.

After a while, Aimee's breathing grew more even, and she relaxed.

Matt lay there, listening to the wind and silently thanking whoever built the shelter for taking the weather patterns up here into consideration. The shelter's solid back wall was turned against the predominant wind direction, which was eastward.

Aimee sighed in her sleep, and half-turned, so that her cheek was no more than an inch from his nose. He could see the faint dusting of freckles on her smooth skin. The scent of lemon and the delicate curve of her cheek made his mouth water. He slid his hand down her arm, doing his best to avoid touching any other part of her. When he reached her wrist, he pressed his fingertips against the silky skin and counted her pulse. It was faint but steady. Then he took her hand in his.

At least her fingers weren't icy cold any more. He sighed in relief. She was warming up. He was pretty sure she was out of danger. But he knew if it had taken them any longer to get here, and if he hadn't been able to get a fire started, she could have died. He breathed deeply and tried to relax. For the moment, they were safe. He needed to get as much rest as he could while he had the chance.

Because tomorrow wasn't going to be easy. Tomorrow, he was going to have to explain to her why they were pressed up against each other and practically naked, why it made sense that he'd brought her up the mountain instead of down, and why he hadn't kept his promise to her—his promise to place William Matthew safely into her arms before the day was out.

CHAPTER 7

AIMEE CAME AWAKE SLOWLY. She was hot. And thirsty. She stirred, trying to push the covers back, but they wouldn't move. Someone was lying very close to her too close. Someone with a very large, very warm body. Her eyes flew open, and she saw the crackling fire in the fireplace.

Fireplace? Where was she? Her pulse thrummed in her throat, and she suddenly felt claustrophobic. She pushed herself up to a sitting position, kicking at the covers and gasping for breath.

"Aimee?"

"Who—?" She dug her heels in and propelled her body backwards, away from whoever was pressing so close against her. She sucked in a huge breath preparing to scream.

"Aimee, it's Matt."

A hand touched her shoulder.

She gasped and coughed.

"Shh. You're okay."

"Matt?" She blinked and looked at the figure that sat up next to her. "Matt? What are you doing —?" She pushed at him.

"Aimee, whoa! You're going to fall off the cot."

He reached out toward her, but she recoiled instinctively. She was in bed—in bed! What kind of crazy dream was she having about Matt, of all people?

"I was just trying to warm you up. You were cold—too cold. I had to get your body temperature up. Do you remember?"

She stared at him, trying to process what he was saying. She couldn't, any more than she could figure out why she was here in this strange, three-sided building next to him. He was bare chested, his skin glowing like gold in the firelight. His dark hair was tousled and wavy, as if he'd just toweled it dry.

She lifted the edge of the covers and looked down at herself. All she had on was a little tank top and panties. "What's going on? Why—?" Had Matt undressed her? She raised her shocked gaze to his and absently registered a look of apology in his expression.

"I had to," he said. "You were freezing."

She stared at him as bits of memories flashed across her brain. Matt wrapping an arm around her and telling her she was going to be okay. Snow blowing in her face, her eyes and lips stinging with cold—the smell of gasoline, the sounds of gunfire. And the awful, menacing words crackling down the phone wire. *If you want to see your baby again...*

If you want to see your baby again— If you want to —"William!" she cried, his name ripping from her throat. Suddenly they were all there. All the memories. All the terror. All the anguish. "My baby! Where is he?"

"Aimee, shh. Try to stay calm."

She heard the words, but hardly registered where they came from. All she knew was that they cut like a razor through her heart.

"Calm? My baby is gone. They stole him, out of his bed." Her hands flew to her mouth. "I was asleep. I was asleep and they took him." Her eyes burned, and her mouth was dry. So dry. She licked her lips.

"You're thirsty. I'll get you some water."

It was Matt, she realized. Will's best friend. *Safe as houses.* But he wasn't. He'd taken Will away from her and let him die. He'd shown up like a knight in shining armor at the very moment when she needed a hero, but he'd let William's kidnapper get away and he didn't save her baby. Pain lanced through her and she clutched at her middle.

When Matt rose, she saw that his lower body was almost as bare as his upper. He was dressed in nothing but snug-fitting boxer briefs. They both were nearly naked. She rubbed her temple, wishing she could put all this information together and come up with a reasonable understanding of what was happening. She did know who he was now. And she knew they hadn't rescued William. But where were they? And how'd they get there?

"I melted some snow, once the fire got going," he said conversationally as he wrapped a blanket around himself. He picked up a metal cup and filled it from a pan that sat near the fireplace.

"Here." He held out the cup.

She couldn't move. She still clutched the covers to her chest like a shield.

"Come on, Aimee, take the cup. You need to drink some water." He pressed the cup into her cool palm.

He turned and went back to the fire, where he picked up pieces of clothing. For the first time, she noticed two straight-backed chairs sitting by the hearth. He piled the clothes on the hearth and spread other pieces over the backs of the chairs. She watched him as she lifted the cup to her lips. The flat, tepid water tasted wonderful. She drank the whole cupful.

"Our clothes will probably be dry by morning."

"Could I have some more?" she asked, and at once felt guilty because she was warm and safe and enjoying water while her baby was out there somewhere—alone. Maybe thirsty. Maybe cold. The pain hit her again, swift and sharp. "Oh—"

Matt took the cup from her hands. "What's wrong? Are you hurting?"

"I want—I need my baby." Tears stung her eyes, but she lifted her chin and swallowed them. "Do you—" She paused, terribly afraid she knew the answer to the question she was about to ask. "Do you know where he is?"

He filled the cup and handed it back to her, then filled another one and drank it himself. He went back to checking and rearranging the clothing. "No. I don't know where he is right now. But the storm is almost over and I'm hoping that by morning the clouds will have cleared away. We'll meet Deke at the rendezvous point, and he can take you back with him. As soon as I find William, I'll—"

"What?" She was still having trouble sorting everything out, but her brain finally put his words together in the proper order. "No!" She slammed the cup down on the wooden floor with a clang. "I am not going back without my baby."

"Aimee, you have to. You can't stay up here. I don't have the supplies or shelter to take care of you."

"Why can't Deke bring us supplies?"

"Because he's going to get you to safety while I rescue William."

He picked up a pair of dark leggings and pulled

them up, then tugged a matching long-sleeved shirt over his head.

"But—"

"Listen to me, Aimee. I can't concentrate on rescuing William and worry about you at the same time." He found her silk long-sleeved top and handed it to her. "Put this on and get back under the covers. It's still a couple of hours until morning. After the snowstorm started, you got hypothermic, so from now on you're going to be susceptible to the cold. You need all the strength you can muster."

She took the shirt and pulled it on. "Don't ignore me, Matt. And don't treat me like I'm going to break. I was confused when I first woke up, but I'm not now." *Not completely.* She smoothed the shirt down over her abdomen. "I can't sleep any more. William is out there. I have to get ready. We have to go find him."

Matt sat on his haunches and tossed back the rest of his water, then sat the cup on the hearth. He picked up a stick and poked the fire. "You need to rest," he said again, not looking at her.

She wanted to be angry at him, needed to be. But his quiet, deliberate actions didn't invite attacks. In fact, his composure was calming.For a moment, she was mesmerized by the silhouette of his profile, outlined by the orange glow from the coals. It was classic and grim. She could believe he was an ancient warrior, staring into the flames as he prepared his mind for battle.

Suddenly, a memory from the night before flashed across her mind. He'd been lying next to her on the cot, his legs and chest pressed against her from behind. She remembered the thick warmth of his skin against hers, the rapid rise and fall of his chest and belly. The feel of his erection, hard and hot against her. And she remembered desire echoing through her like the lyrics of an almost forgotten song. She'd stirred, and he'd backed away with a groan. He'd whispered something. *I promise,* or maybe *I'm sorry.*

It occurred to her that he was in his element here. Weather and survival had been his specialties in the Air Force. There were probably only a handful of people in the world as well trained as Matt to rescue her baby. He hadn't been exaggerating when he said he couldn't take care of her and do his job. She was definitely a liability. She knew that. He couldn't move as fast or as stealthily with her along. He couldn't focus all his concentration and energy on overpowering the kidnapper and rescuing William if he had to be concerned about her safety.

But she was right, too. When he found William, she had to be there. Matt might be the only person she could trust to find her child, but she was the only one who could comfort him.

BY THE TIME they got away from the shelter, it was after 0700 hours. Matt had figured out hours earlier that they were going to miss the 0800 rendezvous point he'd arranged with Deke. To have any chance of making it, they would have had to leave before daylight, while the wet snow was still falling. There was a strong possibility that if Aimee became hypothermic again, she could get frostbite or die.

He'd ventured out of the shelter several times during the night to check the weather. The storm had done exactly what he'd figured it would do. It had moved in ahead of predictions. But what he hadn't expected was the second front that had moved in right behind it. He'd seen the low-pressure system that had been building behind the first. It hadn't looked significant, and it had been hours behind the first, larger storm.

But then the first storm had stalled, hovering over the mountain for hours after its predicted movement eastward. The extra time gave the second storm plenty of time to catch up as well as gain strength. Yesterday's weather forecast had the second storm not moving in for another twelve hours. However, by the time the first storm passed through, the second one was already rolling in. The good news was that it was a weaker front and hadn't dropped nearly as much snow. By 0630, the snow had stopped and the storm was beginning to dissipate. Matt had figured that within another hour, the skies might be clear enough to use his satellite phone.

He'd found a pair of snowshoes in the shelter. He gave them to Aimee, despite her protests. He could survive, even if his feet got wet. She couldn't.

In the place of the snowshoes, the firewood, a liter-sized plastic bottle filled with melted snow, and two of the wool blankets, Matt had left four of his eight remaining fire starters sticks and extra all-weather matches for the next traveler that sought refuge. He figured it was a pretty even exchange.

He'd fashioned one of the blankets into a makeshift pack, tying the corners into knots and using duct tape from his daypack. He carried the makeshift pack containing his electronic devices, the water, the other blanket, and several protein bars, and Aimee carried the daypack with the sleeping bag and the lighter items. He had the heavy machine pistol, and she had the Glock.

"Let's go, Aimee," he called. He'd told her to stay in the shelter until he was sure they were ready to go.

She appeared at the opening, stuffing strands of hair inside the balaclava she'd folded up and donned like a ski cap. Her face was rosy and fresh-looking. Thank God her pallor from the night before was gone.

"You walk in front."

"Are you sure?" she asked. "Wouldn't it be better if you set the pace?"

He looked at her in surprise. "That's a good question."

"You don't have to faint in surprise. I told you, I've done a little hiking in my time."

"Letting me set the pace would be a good idea, if we were evenly matched. But you wouldn't be able to keep up with me. If I lead, I'll be tempted to walk too fast, and then I'll have to slow down to let you catch up. That'll be extremely tiring for me. At the same time, you'll be trying to keep pace when I speed up, which will make you very tired. If you set the pace, you can adjust it to your level of conditioning, and I can find your rhythm. That way we'll both conserve our energy."

Aimee sent him a little smile. "All that and good-looking, too."

His brows rose. She'd surprised him again. "Yeah," he replied. It was good to see her smile. He suspected it was unlikely that she was genuinely amused. She was probably putting on a front, hoping he wouldn't know how scared she was. *Like he could miss it.*

She moved in front of him, a little uncertain balancing on the snowshoes. After the third time she almost stumbled, he called out, "I thought you'd done some hiking."

"I didn't say it was in snow."

He smiled again, and a warmth that had nothing to do with the temperature spread through him. "Now you tell me," he joked as he looked at his watch. By his best calculations, they were about six miles away from where Deke would be circling, looking for them.

Judging by the time they'd made last night, allowing for the fact that they weren't battling a snowstorm and Aimee wasn't hindered by hypothermia this morning, it would still take them at least two hours, maybe more, to get there, trudging through the wet snow. He figured the temperature was about thirty degrees.

And it would rise as the sun rose. While that meant they'd spend the day peeling off layers of clothing so they wouldn't sweat, at least the heat would burn off the rest of the clouds.

Aimee said something that the wind picked up and blew away.

"What?" he called out.

She turned her head. "Do the clouds look like they're thinning? Can you get a signal on your phone?"

He looked up at the clouds that hung heavily above them. They were dissipating toward their rear, to the west. Pulling out the satellite phone, he checked the signal. *Nothing.* "Not yet."

He kept checking over the next hour. Finally, the phone responded with a weak signal. He dialed Irina.

"Matt!" she cried, as soon as she picked up the phone. "What happened? Where are you? Do you have the baby?"

"Not yet. We're headed toward the first rendezvous point, but we're not going to make it on time. Tell Deke we can be there by 1000 hours for sure—"

"Matt, listen. Deke can't make the rendezvous. The helicopter's been sabotaged."

Shock hit his gut. "Repeat. Did you say sabotaged?"

"Affirmative. The fuel line was cut. Deke's working on it."

"I need to get Aimee out of here. Most of my supplies burned up in the Hummer."

"Repeat. I missed that."

"My supplies burned up in the Hummer."

"The Hummer burned? You're on foot?" Irina asked.

"Yeah."

"I understand." Irina said. "Matt, there are—at least two more—"

"Repeat. You're breaking up."

"More storms—this way."

"Right. I'll check it out."

"There's one blowing in now. It'll probably reach Ragged Top within the next two hours."

"Damn," Matt breathed. "Okay. I can deal with the weather. What else?"

"Schiff got an anonymous call this morning. The caller said—Aimee's baby—the Vick cabin. Did —get that?"

"Baby? Cabin?" Matt looked at Aimee. She'd been listening to his side of the conversation the whole time. She met his gaze. He knew shock and relief were plastered all over his face.

Her face lit up, tempered with hesitancy, as if she wasn't quite sure she should actually dare to be excited yet. He nodded at her and smiled as he said, "Got it," to Irina.

"Also gave him the kidna—"

Her voice cut out. "Gave him what?"

"Name. It's Kinnard."

"Kinnard?"

"The police are familiar with him. He's a small-time hood—muscle for some local loan sharks, that sort of thing. And years ago—apparently did some work for Boss—."

"For who?"

"Boss Vick."

That shocked Matt. He turned away from Aimee's curious gaze. For the moment, it might be wise to keep that last tidbit of information to himself.

"Can you verify that?"

"Margo denies—hearing of him, much less knowing —warrant for—papers. But—to take—"

"Irina, I'm losing you. Can Deke make the Sunday rendezvous?"

"Affirma—get in—pick up—Sunday 0900."

"Got it. Sunday 0900. Thanks. Out." Matt disconnected, and then tried to access the weather reports via satellite. But the cloud cover was getting thicker, and reception was spotty. He'd have to continue to rely on old-fashioned methods of reading the weather and predicting what would happen next.

"Matt?" Aimee had waited patiently while he talked to Irina, but he could see that she was bursting with curiosity. "Did she say baby? At the cabin?" she asked hesitantly.

"Someone called in an anonymous tip this morning, letting the FBI know that your baby, your William, is there."

"He's there? At the cabin? Oh—" Aimee capped a hand over her mouth. Her eyes glittered with unshed tears. "Oh, Matt. Do you think the caller was telling the truth? Do you really think he's all right?"

Matt nodded. "From what Irina said, it sounds like he's fine."

She pressed her fingertips to her lips for a few seconds, then ran toward him. Before he realized what she was doing, she slammed into him, wrapping her arms around his neck and hugging him tighter than he'd ever been hugged in his life. He stood there for a second, unsure how to react. But her joy, her relief, her sheer happiness at knowing her child was safe began to seep in past his reserve. Finally, he wrapped his arms around her and hugged her back.

She buried her face in the hollow between his neck and shoulder and hung on. After a few seconds, he realized he felt tears against his neck. "Hey," he said, gently pushing her away and peering at her. "Are you okay?"

She nodded as tears flowed down her cheeks and ran over the corner of her mouth. She sniffed and a smile tugged at her lips. "I'm so relieved. I was so scared."

His heart was twisting again. He'd never known an internal organ could warp in so many different directions. "I know you were. I don't think I've ever seen you cry."

She swiped her fingers across her cheeks. "I don't. Ever."

"I guess this is a pretty special occasion, then."

Her smile broadened, and she laughed. "I guess it is a special occasion." She blew out a breath of air, wiped her cheeks again, and then straightened and looked him in the eye. "I'm not going to do that again. So how far are we from the cabin? How fast can we get there? Who's there with him?"

"Whoa," Matt said, holding up his hands. "I can't tell you who's with him, but I can tell you that we're about ten miles from the cabin and we can get there in four or five hours. But only if you turn around and walk."

She grinned at him. "Which direction?"

The maps he'd memorized suddenly went completely out of his head, knocked out by the dazzle of her grin. He'd seen it before, of course, seen it a lot in all the time he'd known her, but it had been a long time. And very seldom solely at him.

"Hang on a minute," he croaked, holding up a hand. He pulled his glove off with his teeth and retrieved the printed maps from his pocket. After a little shuffling, he came up with the right one. "Okay. Bear eighteen degrees north of east."

"Bear what?"

He laughed ruefully, held up the compass and took the reading, then pointed. "Go thataway."

She turned and looked. "Thataway."

He shook his head. "Walk!"

With a swish of her hips, Aimee turned and started walking.

Matt stuffed his maps back into his pocket and tugged on his glove, looking down at his feet and lecturing himself about how uncool it was to be lusting after his best friend's widow. Especially here. Especially now. They were in a dangerous situation. His job was to take care of her, to protect her. Getting emotional led to screwups. He knew that from personal experience.

Twenty years ago, he, Deke, Rook and Will had found themselves trapped on a mountain ledge when a storm blew in. He'd been the youngest of the four, and the most scared. Rook and Deke, and even Will, only two months older than him, had stayed calm. But he'd sobbed as the reclusive Vietnam veteran Arlis Hanks had pulled him up using a rope and a block and tackle. That was the last time he'd cried. Shaking his head at the memory, Matt looked up.

Aimee was nowhere in sight.

CHAPTER 8

"Aimee!" Matt shouted. "Aimee!" His heart slammed against his chest wall, ripping the breath from his lungs.

He broke into a run. The terrain here was fairly even, and the trees were sparse. He could see for several yards. How could she have disappeared?

God, please don't let her have fallen over a ledge. That thought stopped him in his tracks as alarm sheared his breath. He had to stay calm. Cool. Rational.

The words echoed in his head with each cautious step he took. Combined with deep, even breaths, they helped to slow his pounding heart. He placed his feet into her snowshoe prints. Within about ten paces, he saw the indented ribbon of snow that marked a creek bed. Had she fallen in? "Aimee!" he shouted desperately.

"Matt! Here!" Her voice was shrill with fear.

"Stay still. I'll be right there." He could see the hole in the snow. He approached carefully.

Several feet from the place where Aimee had fallen, he lowered himself to hands and knees and crawled until he could peer over the edge.

Aimee was sitting in a pile of snow.

"Aimee? Don't move. Are you all right?"

She looked up. "Yes," she said disgustedly. "My butt hurts, but not as much as my pride." She moved to stand.

"Wait. Are you sure you're okay? Nothing's sprained? Wrists? Ankles?"

She shook her head. "I've checked everything. I didn't move because I didn't know how I was going to get back up there."

Matt laughed. "That's easy," he said, and proceeded to show her just how easy it was. Back on high ground and standing beside Matt, Aimee brushed snow off her pants as she surveyed the place where she'd fallen. "What did I fall into?"

"A creek bed, and not even a very deep one." He pointed behind them and then in front, tracing the creek's meandering path to where it disappeared among the evergreen trees. "See that narrow ribbon of snow that's kind of sunken?"

"Oh. I should have seen that. It might have saved me a sore butt. All that extra snow blew into the creek? It sort of collects it, I guess."

"That's exactly right. Spend much time hiking in the snow and you learn to notice things you might otherwise not. Little signs, like that dip in the snow, or a shadow that might indicate a rock. Things that can hurt you or even kill you if you don't pay attention."

"Okay, so tell me again why I'm leading, if you're the expert?" She grinned at him.

NOT EVEN HER fall could spoil Aimee's good mood. She felt like laughing and running and dancing. In a little while, she would have her baby back in her arms, safe and sound. That was worth every minute of the previous day. Every second.

Matt's brows drew down. "Good point," he said. "Okay. I'll take the lead, but you've got to keep up. Tell me if I go too fast."

"Okay, sir," she said. "You go in front, and I'll follow. But please, keep showing me the secrets the snow is covering up. Never know when it might come in handy."

Before they headed out again, Matt shed his parka and stuffed it inside his makeshift pack. The snow clinging to his snug-fitting wool sweater glistened in the sunlight. Wool was too fuzzy to clearly outline the muscles in his arms and torso, but Aimee hadn't forgotten how he had looked with the firelight glinting off the planes and angles of his naked torso last night. Nor had she forgotten how his warm, strong body felt pressed against her.

Will had been good-looking, with his light brown hair, his hazel eyes, and dimples that had driven all the high school girls crazy. He was always voted most handsome and most likely to succeed. He'd been big and tall, and captain of the football team.

Matt, on the other hand, had once been voted most shy. His dark hair, brown eyes, and strong features weren't as classically handsome as Will's had been. His nose was a little too long, and he'd never played football. He'd been on the swim team. His muscles had always been long and lean. In fact, some had considered him downright skinny. But after last night, Aimee had decided Matt was a dangerously attractive and sexy man.

"Okay, let's go," he said, sending her a puzzled look. "You sure you're okay?"

She nodded and shrugged her shoulders to seat the daypack into a comfortable position. As she moved into step behind him, she considered her thoughts. She was sure she'd seen him in a bathing suit, back in high school and college. She was positive she had. She and Will and Matt had all gone down to Florida on spring break one year, and they'd all stayed in the same room. But she hardly remembered Matt at all. What she remembered about that trip was that she and Will had sex for the first time. In the hotel room—with Matt asleep on the other bed.

Her cheeks burned. What had she been thinking? Granted it was years ago, probably long forgotten by Matt, if he'd even woken up, but still— how embarrassing.

And now, after having spent the night before pressed against his lean hard body, thinking about that long-ago experience kind of turned her on. Guilt brought heat to her cold cheeks. *Stop it.*

Matt held up a hand. "Shh."

She froze.

He sent her a quick look over his shoulder, and then cocked his head, listening.

Before she realized that he'd moved, Matt had grabbed her arm and pulled her toward him. He propelled her over to a stand of trees and followed her several feet in, until they were surrounded by trees on all sides. Then he crouched down, and pulled her back between his knees.

"Stay quiet," he whispered in her ear.

"What is—?"

He put his fingers across her mouth. She nodded against them, and after a couple of seconds, he removed them. For a long time, they crouched there, spooned awkwardly. Even through layers of clothes, the sense of intimacy was as strong as it had been the night before.

Her insides stirred, tingling with sensations that she hadn't felt in a long time. She yearned to lean back, to press herself against Matt the way he'd pressed his body against hers last night. Her eyes drifted closed as the tingling centered itself in her core.

He put his hands on her shoulders. She wanted to cover them with hers, to take them and pull them around her, so she could feel like she'd felt last night. As much as it scared her to admit that she wanted him, that was how much she longed for him to touch her, to kiss her, and yes, even to make love with her. She told herself it was because he made her feel safe.

His fingers squeezed her shoulders, massaging them. He leaned forward, his breath warming her cheek. Was he feeling the same thing she was? Then she heard it. A buzzing sound. Very faint. She turned her head, but she couldn't tell where it was coming from. What was it? An engine?

Her pulse sped up. An engine. A helicopter! Maybe it was Deke, coming to rescue them. He could take them to the Vick's cabin and help them rescue William. Her breath caught in an excited sob. But if it were Deke's helicopter, why were they hiding?

"Is that an engine?" she whispered.

Matt put his ear next to hers and nodded his head.

"Helicopter?" she asked hopefully.

He shook his head. "Snowmobile."

Snowmobile? That could be anybody. "Oh."

He pressed his fingertips against her lips again, warning her to stay quiet. Slowly, over what seemed to be an endless stretch of time, the noise of the engine grew louder. It kept growing louder, until it sounded like it was close enough to run them down.

Matt put his hand on the back of her head. "Put your head down. And don't move."

As she lowered her head, Matt pressed his forehead against her back. She could imagine what the two of them looked like. Two small, fragile humans dwarfed by the tall trees, crouched together, hoping and praying that they couldn't be seen by someone whizzing by on a snowmobile. Or someone searching for them—

Her heart pounded so loudly she was afraid it could be heard over the motor's noise.

As the engine noise grew deafening, she felt Matt straighten. He left his hand resting gently on the back of her neck so she didn't budge. He grew so still that if it weren't for the slow, steady rise and fall of his chest, she might be able to forget he was there, pressed against her. Okay, that was not true. She wouldn't forget the feeling of his body molded to hers—not for a very long time.

Finally, the noise of the engine faded into the

distance. Aimee waited until Matt took his hand away from the nape of her neck before she sat up.

"Ah," she moaned as her muscles relaxed from their cramped position. She looked at Matt. "Who was it? Could you see anything?"

He nodded grimly.

"Was it the kidnapper?"

"Nope. It was Al Hamir. There was a lot of blood on his pants. The kidnapper must have shot him in the side. He didn't look happy, but he didn't look like he was too slowed down, either."

"He didn't see us." She phrased it as a statement, but she watched Matt's face. "Where do you think he's going?"

He rubbed his thumb across his lower lip and averted his gaze. "I'm afraid he's probably headed for the cabin, just like we are."

And as quickly as that, all sense of confidence and joy at the knowledge that William was only a few miles away and safe dissolved, and Aimee was back in that awful place where she'd existed since six-thirty Wednesday morning.

"Why?" she moaned. "I thought you didn't think he was connected with the kidnapping. How would he know about the cabin?"

Matt's jaw clenched. After an instant of wavering, his gaze met hers. "All I can figure out is that both he and Kinnard are—"

"Kinnard?" She'd never heard that name before.

She didn't like how Matt was acting. "Who is Kinnard?"

"That's the kidnapper's name."

"The man who took William?" *Kinnard.* A name. A real person on which to focus blame. "Who is he?"

"According to the FBI, he's a small-time criminal that has operated around the Crook County area for the past twenty years or so."

"Why would he take William Matthew?"

Matt straightened. "We should get going."

"No. You should tell me what's going on. Who is Kinnard, and what are you trying so hard not to tell me?"

"I think both men are working for Novus Ordo."

"Novus Ordo? The terrorist?" She felt the blood drain from her face. She'd thought nothing could be as bad as having her baby kidnapped. But by terrorists?

"You're talking about Novus Ordo?" she asked. "The man whose face nobody has ever seen? The one they say is worse than Bin Laden?"

Matt swallowed and reluctantly met her gaze. "We believe he had Rook assassinated because Rook saw him. He may be the only person outside Novus's inner circle who has ever seen the man's face."

"I don't—understand." What did Rook Castle

and an infamous terrorist have to do with her? With her baby? But she was terribly afraid she did understand.

"It's complicated. But the theory is that since Rook's body was never recovered, and since Irina has been searching for him all this time, Novus has been watching her, just in case."

"In case Rook is still alive." Aimee couldn't believe she was hearing—much less understanding—what Matt was saying.

Matt nodded. "Since security is so tight around Castle Ranch that Irina and Deke are virtually untouchable, Novus is trying to capture me, to interrogate me about Rook."

"A terrorist kidnapped my baby to get to you? I *knew* it! I knew my baby's kidnapping had something to do with you." She stood and turned away from him.

"I'm not positive, but if Kinnard is working for Novus, and if the anonymous caller was telling the truth—"

"Then the cabin is a trap. Oh." Aimee's heart felt ripped to shreds. She put her gloved hands to her mouth and breathed into them, trying to stop the panic rising in her throat. She spoke, her words muffled by the thick gloves. "Of course it is. We can't go to the cabin." She swallowed panic and fear and breathed in courage. "They'll capture you."

Matt rose and faced her. He took her hands

away from her mouth and held them. "I made you a promise. Nothing—nothing is going to stop me from keeping it."

Her breath hitched.

"Everything we know points to William being at the cabin. We're going."

"REMEMBER WHAT I TOLD YOU," Matt said.

Aimee barely heard him. It had taken four hours, but they were finally looking down at the cabin from their vantage point on a rise to the west. She stared at the primitive log structure. She knew a little about it from Will. His father, Boss Vick, had spent an obscene amount of money to equip the simple dwelling.

He'd brought a crew up one summer who'd cleared trees, installed a generator, and carted appliances and furniture up. He'd made it into a comfortable winter retreat, if one didn't mind skiing in, or living with the prospect of being snowed in.

Aimee had always thought the idea of spending so much on a hunting shack was wasteful, but right now, the amenities sounded wonderful to her—the generator, the appliances, the comfortable furnishings—because they meant that her baby was warm and comfortable and well-fed—and in the hands of terrorists.

"Aimee? Did you hear me?"

She nodded. "I don't make a move until you've gone down there and verified that nobody is waiting to shoot us when we step out into the open." She couldn't take her eyes off the house. She squinted, but couldn't see through any of the windows. But that was okay. Whether she could see him or not, her baby was in there. Her fingers itched—her arms ached—to hold him.

But Matt was right. They had to take precautions. There were at least two people on this mountain who meant them harm.

"You'll wave all clear, and motion me to come down. Or you'll hold up your hands palm down and press them down, meaning stay where I am." She demonstrated what he'd shown her earlier.

"Good. And if something happens to me?"

She pressed her lips together and squeezed her eyes shut. "I run for the cabin."

"Have you been to the cabin before?" he asked.

"No."

Matt nodded. "Okay. I've been a couple of times. I think I remember the layout."

"Matt, I'm worried. Maybe this is not a good idea. Maybe we ought to wait until Deke gets here. Spend the night up here in this shelter, or—" She wanted to cry. It nearly killed her to suggest waiting. She thought she would die if she had to wait one second longer to hold her baby, but the prospect of Matt being captured by terrorists—captured and interrogated—was nearly as horrible to contemplate as the possibility that she might never see William again.

"No." He shook his head, dislodging snowflakes from his hair. He held out his gloved hand and several more fell onto it. "See that? It's starting to snow again. The storms we just went through last night are only the beginning. There are more stacked up, waiting for their shot at us. And we have no shelter." He craned his neck and examined the sky. "There's a very good chance that we wouldn't survive the night. With just the mummy bag for the two of us, it's too risky. Getting to the cabin is our best chance."

"What if we both go down at the same time? We can watch each other's backs. You'll have that machine gun thing, and I have the Glock. We can hold them off."

His face softened into an almost-smile. "Or . . . we could wait until right before nightfall. We could probably sit out a storm during the day without freezing to death. Even behind the clouds, the sun still provides a lot of heat. Whoever's down there might not expect us to wait until dark."

"Okay," Aimee said hesitantly. "But what will we do until then?"

Matt kept his gaze on the cabin and the surrounding area. "We need to get to work if we're going to spend the rest of the day here. I want to build a snow shelter. It'll hide us and keep us warm after the clouds roll in. Plus it'll protect us from the snow and the wind." He peered through the trees at the cabin, then scanned the tree line above and below the clearing. "I don't see anyone. Al Hamir and Kinnard both are probably right at home on the mountain, and I know Al Hamir is trained in guerilla tactics. We don't want to be seen, so we have to work quickly and at the same time stay hidden. Be prepared to crawl around."

"What do you need me to do?" She recognized his Special Forces voice and that serious expression that made her think he was ready for anything.

He sent her a glance that cemented her belief that the only thoughts in his head were how to carry out the mission successfully. "Keep an eye on the cabin while I scout around for the best place to locate our shelter. I like the look of that overhanging rock over there. We need to hurry, though. From the looks of the sky, by the time we get the shelter built, we're going to be very glad to have it."

SURE ENOUGH, by the time the shelter was ready, the new storm had rolled in, bringing another sky full of heavy, snow-laden clouds and a nasty mixture of freezing rain and snow.

Aimee sat inside the cramped space, waiting for Matt to come inside. He'd spread a space blanket on the ground and folded one of the blankets on top of it. He'd covered the downhill side of the lean-to with the other blanket, and it made a huge difference in the inside temperature.

Matt pushed aside the blanket and climbed inside, bringing freezing air and icy spray with him. He'd put his parka back on while building the shelter. Now he draped it over the makeshift back-pack. "Not bad, if I do say so. What do you think?"

She tried to smile, but she knew she wasn't pulling it off. "Better than the Ritz."

"Hey," he said, his voice closer than she'd expected. It was nearly pitch black with the blanket closed. And granted, the entire space of the shelter was about six feet by three feet. Still, she'd figured he'd hover near one side and she'd cling to the other.

"How're you doing? It'll be dark within about three hours. Then we can sneak down to the cabin and check things out. Meanwhile, you should take off your parka. Believe it or not, it'll be easier to adjust to the temperature without it on. Plus when we get ready to go, you'll be glad you have another layer to put on."

Aimee carefully shrugged out of the down

jacket. She held onto it and used it to cover her hands. She'd taken off her gloves, which were wet from piling and packing snow.

"Matt, can I ask you a question?"

"Sure. Anything."

"You said Irina and Deke were untouchable because of the security around the ranch."

"Right. Rook installed the best equipment money could buy. And all the employees are screened carefully."

"But when you were talking to Irina, you mentioned sabotage. Wasn't that at the ranch?"

He stared at her for a moment. "I did. Somebody tampered with Deke's helicopter. Irina said it was definitely sabotage." He cursed. "I was so focused on how soon Deke could get up here that the idea of a security breach didn't sink in. Irina could be in danger." He shook his head.

"You're awfully hard on yourself."

"What?"

Aimee sent him a small smile. "You're out here, protecting me, and doing your best to rescue my baby, but at the same time you're beating yourself up for not thinking about Irina's possible danger."

He shrugged. "I feel responsible."

"I know you do. It's the kind of man you are." She settled against the rock that formed the back of their lean-to. "From everything I know about Deke, I'm guessing he can protect her."

"Yeah. He can."

For several minutes, they sat silently. Aimee could feel Matt's tension. Was he still kicking himself? She figured it was time to change the subject.

She looked around at the shelter he'd built. "I guess this is how the first Americans lived for hundreds of years."

"Thousands. Yeah. We're soft these days."

"Not you," she said, poking his bicep with her finger.

He laughed, a soft rumbling sound. "Yeah, me."

She lay her hand on his arm. "Not you," she murmured.

His gaze snapped to hers. Even in the near blackness, his dark eyes picked up a reflection from somewhere, and in that reflection was the thing that had been born of their necessary closeness in the shelter the night before. The awareness that they were not just two people bound by their love for his friend and her husband.

Aimee cringed at what she'd done. One poke might have been just an innocent gesture. One teasing touch could be ascribed to friendship. But she'd touched him twice. She'd lingered. That was no innocent gesture.

After the awkward silence had swelled to uncomfortable proportions, he uttered a small chuckle. "Oh? Well, what about you? You aren't looking so bad." He slid his hand along the line of her shoulder and upper arm. "A little on the skinny side."

That was all he did. Yet her body burned as if he'd trailed hot fingers over its entire length.

"My guess is you've got some fair-sized biceps yourself."

Aimee moistened her lips. Innocent teasing, she told herself. That's all it was. How long had it been since she'd felt like laughing even a little bit, other than when she played with William. Besides, she'd known Matt for most of her life. He was a friend.

There might be a smidgen of sexual tension between them, the natural attraction between a man and a woman who are forced together by circumstance. That's all this was.

Natural. Understandable. Easily ignored. What could a little teasing hurt? It was better than sitting here in gloomy silence for hours. A little humor would help pass the time. She squeezed her fist and flexed her arm muscles. "Fair-sized bicep? I beg your pardon. Check this out."

His fingers closed around her bicep—it felt like they completely circled her upper arm. "Yeah," he said softly. "You're a regular American Ninja Warrior."

His breath fanned her cheek. He was that close. Aimee had no idea what to do next. Apparently he did, however. He let go of her arm and slid his hand around her shoulders.

"Here." His voice rumbled through her like the purr of a lion. "We can keep each other warm." His arm was firm and big and comforting, and his body radiated heat. Aimee was tempted to tuck herself into the warm safe nook created by his torso and arm. He pulled her closer.

She sighed and gave in to temptation, relaxing against him. His breaths ruffled her hair. She raised her head, wanting to feel his breath on her skin. When she did, her nose brushed his chin, and she breathed in his scent. He smelled of snow and evergreen, with a hint of smokiness. It plummeted her back to the night before and his warm embrace. Her breath caught.

He uttered a small moan, deep in his throat, and then pressed his forehead against hers and slid his fingers up her shoulder to cradle the back of her head. "Aimee—"

Her heart fluttered—from fear or desire, she wasn't sure. She had no idea what he was going to do or say. She had no idea what she wanted him to do or say. As far as she was concerned, they could sit like this for the next three hours. She was pretty sure that three hours of Matt's full attention would bolster not only her courage, but her energy and her resolve as well.

"Aimee, I need to tell you something."

She rolled her forehead from side to side against his. "No, you don't." *Don't ruin this moment with reality*. Don't make it anything more than it is. A stolen instant out of time.

"I do. I need to expl—"

She kissed him—just grabbed his face between her hands and—smack. No hesitation, no nips or teases or nibbles. Just a full-on, openmouthed kiss. She did it because, despite the fact that they were sitting here in this dangerous, tense situation, pursued by men who could be working for the most ruthless terrorist on the planet, waiting for nightfall so they could rescue her seven-month-old baby, she felt safe and secure. The last thing she wanted was for him to jerk her back to reality with guilt-ridden explanations of why he didn't go to Will's funeral, or come back for William's christening.

She knew how guilty and responsible he felt. She knew because he was that kind of man. He took the heat, the hits, the blame. Not in some arrogant, look-how-great-I-am way either. When he succeeded, he did so quietly, without fanfare. When he failed, he handled that quietly as well.

By the time that thought had flitted through her head, Matt was returning her kiss as fully and enthusiastically as she'd kissed him. He didn't waste any time hesitating, or testing her reaction. He kissed her, and she discovered that beneath Matt's ordinary-guy veneer ran an undercurrent of passion, need, and sexual hunger far greater than she'd imagined. His heart beat strongly, rapidly, vibrating through her as his mouth moved over hers with authority and exquisite gentleness.

A thrill of unexpectedly strong desire pulsed through her all the way to her core. She leaned closer, yielding to the promise of his kiss, but then he stopped. He lifted his head and hovered there, his lips so close to hers that their warmth still lingered on her mouth.

"Matt?"

He was frowning, his eyes as black as coals. "What are we doing?" he whispered.

CHAPTER 9

A TWINGE of uncertainty embedded itself beneath Aimee's breastbone at Matt's question. *Don't ask what we're doing,* she wanted to say. *Don't make it more than it is—or less.* She didn't have the courage to say that, so she tried to make light of it. "Staying warm?" Her eyes had adjusted to the darkness so that she saw the uncertainty in his expression.

He smiled, but the worry didn't leave his eyes. His gaze roamed over her face, as if he were searching for something. "I'd really like to talk to you about—"

Aimee put her fingers over his mouth. "Please don't. Not now. I need to concentrate on William."

"Sure. Of course." He pulled away. "Sorry."

"Don't do that. Don't get all honorable and responsible on me."

"I'm confused," he said. "I'm not sure what you want from me."

She took a deep breath. "I'm tired and cold and scared, and I'm feeling very alone." She nibbled on her lower lip for a second. "Is it possible I want the same thing from you that you want from me?"

Matt's eyes widened, and then narrowed. He sat unmoving for a moment, and then touched her chin with his forefinger. "I never meant to come on to you. I didn't intend to let this happen."

"I know that. Me either. But it's happening." She looked at his lips. "At least it is for me."

"Aimee—"

She looked at him from under her lashes, hearing his unspoken plea. "Just hold me for a little while. Hold me and keep me warm."

"No problem," he said with a sigh. "No problem at all." He settled back against the rock and cradled her against his side. His other hand held her head against his chest, and she felt him press a sweet kiss against her hair.

She could hear his heartbeat, steady and fast. After a few moments, Aimee felt his thumb sliding across her cheek in a rhythmic, sweet caress. She sighed and curled her fingers against his chest. When she did, his heart sped up and his breaths turned ragged. He stiffened, and she knew he was becoming aroused. If she stirred, or if he did, she'd find out for sure just how turned on he was. It surprised her just how much she wanted to find out.

She knew Matt almost as well as she'd known her own husband. Probably better than any other man she'd ever known. She knew he wanted her. His body told her that. But she also knew he would never act on those feelings. Matt valued honor and loyalty above all else. In his mind, acting on sexual feelings for his best friend's widow would be a betrayal of her trust in him.

If she left it up to him, the stolen kiss and this warm embrace were as far as he would go. But even if she regretted it later, right now she wasn't willing to stop. Heaven help her, she wanted more. Much more. The thought of touching him sent a thrill of desire humming through her. Her breath caught and her pulse raced. She turned her head and pressed a soft kiss to the sensitive underside of his chin, feeling a triumphant satisfaction when he gasped quietly. Then she shifted, to gain easier access to his mouth. For an instant, he sat still and unyielding, but she persisted, kissing his mouth and cheek, wrapping her arms around his neck.

He dragged her across his lap and gave her back kiss for kiss, caress for caress, until both of them were out of breath. Matt lifted her and somehow she ended up lying on her back with him hovering over her. After a searching look, he lowered his head and kissed her again.

She didn't remember ever experiencing anything like the feeling of his mouth on hers, of his body pressed against hers. He was aggressive and gentle at the same time. Demanding and giving. He rested his weight on his elbows so he could look at her. His erection pulsed against her thigh.

She slid her hand down his ridged abdomen until her palm found his hardness. The feel of his erection, firm and vibrant against her fingers, even through the barrier of his clothes, sent desire thrumming through her like a drumbeat. He shuddered, and she knew he was almost to the edge. He felt for the buttons on her pants while at the same time his tongue slid over the sensitive skin of her neck. When his teeth scraped her earlobe and his breath warmed her ear, her entire body contracted in erotic reaction.

She opened her pants with his help and shivered as his cool hand slid inside the waistband of her underwear. Before he even touched her, she was gasping for breath. Then his fingers reached their goal. She cried out.

He stopped, but she moaned in protest. "Matt, please. I need to feel you, too."

His dark eyes searched her face. Then he sat up, loosened his pants, and stretched his length against her again.

Her backside was cold, pressed against the poor

insulation of a thin blanket, but Matt's legs, his torso, his groin, radiated warmth. His erection, hard against her, burned her skin with a delicious heat that turned her insides to liquid fire.

She closed her fingers around him, feeling his velvety hardness jump in her hand. At the same time, his fingers slid gently along the folds that hid her center. She arched, the pleasure almost painful in its intensity. Pleasure she hadn't felt for far too long.

He teased her there, circling and coaxing, dipping and withdrawing, again and again, as his mouth traveled from her neck to her collarbone and on, to find the tip of her breast and nip at it through the layers of her clothing.

Then he lifted himself and settled between her thighs. His rigid shaft rubbed against her, driving her desire. She opened to him, oblivious of the chilled air and the icy cold ground.

Bending his head, he nibbled at her lips, then pulled back and looked into her eyes. "You okay?" he whispered.

In answer, she arched her neck and reached for his mouth with hers. "I'm ready," she whispered against his lips, knowing that he would know that within a second. Her core was liquefying, flowing, preparing to receive him. He looked deeply into her eyes as if searching for something, then with deliberate, torturous slowness, he sank into her.

She moaned as his full length filled her and exquisite longing spread like golden, fluid light through her body. Enveloped in a haze of erotic sensation, all she could do was feel.

He stayed there, buried in her, his face tucked into the hollow between her neck and shoulder, for an interminable time. The feel of his breath on her neck was, if possible, more intimate than the sensation of his hardness filling her. It was a gesture of surrender, of trust, she realized.

He was blind with his eyes tucked into her flesh. He was vulnerable with his neck exposed to possible enemies. He was open, undefended. Her eyes filled with tears. She slid her hand around the nape of his neck, and turned her face toward his.

Then he moved, and her body spasmed, sending electric shocks of pleasure tumbling through her. He slid out, until he hovered at her opening, then in to fill her again. The slow friction increased her wetness and made each successive thrust easier. Each time he pushed into her, he sped up slightly, his body coaxing hers to keep pace with him. Then he slowed, staying suspended above her for a long time, watching her. She realized he was gauging her response and tailoring his movements to hers.

When she thought she would burst with anticipation, when her breasts were puckered and tight and her entire body felt electrified with reaction, he sat back on his haunches and pulled her legs atop his thighs. Then he held onto her waist and thrust again and again, filling her more completely and more deeply than she'd ever imagined possible. Faster, deeper, so erotic and so loving.

At last, he wrapped his arms around her and lifted her upright. He held here there, suspended, until she whimpered with need, then lowered her onto him. His powerful thighs flexed as he thrust upward.

Aimee gasped and cried out as a place inside her that had never been touched shattered. Matt kissed her, swallowing her breathless cries. Then he came too, violently and thoroughly, his jaw clenched and his eyes squeezed shut as he poured everything he had into her. With one last powerful thrust, he rocked with her and against her, continuing the dance as their climax faded.

After a few seconds of sitting there, draped against each other in the afterglow of sexual fulfillment, he splayed his fingers over her back again and gently lowered her to the ground, following her and settling beside her.

She laid her head on his shoulder as tears filled her eyes and ran over the bridge of her nose.

He touched one with his thumb and wiped it away. "What's happening here?" he said tenderly. "Is something wrong?"

She shook her head slightly. "No. Nothing."

He kissed her forehead while his thumb swirled

over her skin, spreading and dissipating the dampness. "Are you sure? Because I'm pretty sure I see a tear. Why?"

She shrugged and bit her lip to keep from saying, *Because this is a special occasion.*

MATT WOKE up cold and stiff. Something sharp was poking him in the back. Something soft and sweet-smelling was pressed against his chest and side. He'd been dreaming about Aimee.

Aimee. He opened his eyes and discovered that his dream had come true. She was asleep with her head on his chest. Her brown hair was wavy and soft, and it tickled his nose. He'd kissed that hair, that brow, those lips. He'd—his body shuddered with a small aftershock of his explosive orgasm. What the hell had he been thinking? Embarrassment and chagrin sent heat up his neck to burn his face. *You're a first-class asshole, Parker.*

Carefully, he lifted his arm and glanced at his watch. Almost seven. They'd slept for over two hours. The realization disturbed him. He'd left himself—and more importantly Aimee—vulnerable and exposed. The makeshift shelter was a pathetic cover. Had anyone happened by, they'd have been caught or killed. He lay still for a moment and listened. He heard nothing but the wind whistling through the naked tree branches, and the muffled whisper of falling snow. Occasionally, he heard a branch crack and fall, weighted down by snow and ice.

Aimee stirred and murmured something in her sleep. Matt ran his palm lightly down her arm as his heart squeezed in regret. He'd done worse than leave her vulnerable by falling asleep on watch. He'd taken advantage of her by making love with her. She was completely dependent on him to keep her safe. She was frightened for her baby. And he'd promised to take care of her. Instead, he'd let his feelings get involved. He'd acted on his personal desire, and put her in danger. *Another promise broken.*

Despite his self-recrimination, his brain replayed the highlights of those few stolen moments and the way she opened to him as he sank hilt-deep inside her.

To his dismay, his erection grew and strained from just the thought of making love with her. It was a physical symbol of his betrayal. He'd always been afraid that she or Will or someone who knew them would see the truth in his face—how smitten he'd always been with her. He'd never even admitted to himself how much he'd wanted her. Until now. He closed his eyes and clenched his jaw, forcing his brain back to his mission.

Carefully, he slid his arm from around her and sat up.

She stirred again, so he pulled the corner of the mummy bag over his lap to hide his erection, disgusted with himself.

She opened her eyes and looked at him in sleepy confusion. Then her eyes widened. He stared, mesmerized by the myriad emotions that flitted across her features. To his surprise, she didn't turn away in disgust, or scream for help. Finally, she scraped her lower lip with her teeth and dropped her gaze. Embarrassed? Humiliated? Afraid?

"Aimee, I'm sorry."

Her eyes snapped back up to lock with his. "Sorry?"

He nodded miserably. "We need to dress. It's getting dark, and I want to watch the cabin for a while before we make our move."

She shivered, and then ducked her head, searching around the cramped space for her clothes.

Matt turned the other way and dressed. Then he checked his MAC-10 to be sure it hadn't gotten wet, and loaded it. He did the same with the Glock and handed it to Aimee, handle first.

"Remember. From this point on, there's a chance you'll have to shoot someone to save your life or William's. You have to decide now whether you can do it. Don't aim if you're not prepared to shoot. And don't shoot if you're not prepared to kill."

She nodded, accepting the gun and sliding it into the paddle holster she'd already put on. As soon as she'd finished dressing, she started rolling up the blankets. Matt stuffed them into his home-made pack and then took the mummy bag's stuff sack from Aimee and packed it.

The sound of a motor starting up echoed across the snow. He froze, listening. The motor revved once, twice. He touched Aimee's arm. "Stay right here."

"Matt—"

"Stay here, and don't make a sound."

He carefully pushed the blanket aside and slipped out. When he'd sneaked as close to the edge of the overhang as he dared go, he used his eyes like an eagle or a hawk would to strafe the ground and search for prey.

Down below, Kinnard was on the snowmobile. As he watched, Kinnard revved it again, then turned off the engine. He cursed as he climbed off the vehicle and stomped back toward the cabin. Had he forgotten something?

Without moving a muscle he didn't need, Matt groped in his backpack until his hand closed around his binoculars. He pulled them out and watched Kinnard mount the snow-covered steps.

As the kidnapper reached for the door handle, a

loud crack rang out, practically over Matt's head. Kinnard whirled and looked in their direction. Matt didn't move. A huge branch crashed noisily as it fell through lower branches. It hit the ground not ten feet away from him with a deafening thud.

Kinnard stood perfectly still, watching and listening. His head was raised, and his gaze was on the trees that were still swaying as they rebounded from being hit by the falling branch. Matt knew that where he sat was partially obscured by tangled underbrush. He also knew that if he moved, Kinnard's brain would separate his gray and green and white camo from the surrounding natural foliage.

Behind him, he heard Aimee stirring. It took every ounce of willpower he possessed not to move or speak. *Stay still, Aimee.*

Matt didn't take his eyes off Kinnard as the man squinted up at the place where the branch had fallen. Behind him, Aimee continued to move. If she decided to push the blanket aside, they'd be sitting ducks.

Finally, the kidnapper's rigid stance relaxed. He glanced around, then went inside the cabin. Matt didn't dare move. If Kinnard was just retrieving something he'd forgotten, he'd be out within seconds. Sure enough, Kinnard appeared again almost immediately. He climbed on the snowmobile, started it up, and headed northeast. Matt got a glimpse of the rifle in its scabbard attached to the right side of the vehicle.

His breath hissed out between his teeth. He lifted the binoculars again and examined every inch of the cabin. As he was studying the layout and trying to remember anything he could about the couple of trips he and Will made up here when they were kids, a dim light came on in one of the windows. His pulse sped up as a young woman appeared, holding a baby. She was rocking from one foot to another and bouncing the boy in her arms. As he watched, she bent her head and kissed him on his forehead.

A frisson of relief slithered down his spine. The woman's stance and demeanor were that of a caregiver. A nanny maybe. Or a mother. She was obviously caring for William. Aimee's baby was in safe hands—for the moment.

He sent up a brief prayer of thanks as he turned his gaze back to the northeast. The hum of the snowmobile's motor was waning. Kinnard was gone, at least for a while.

They needed to make their move now. He detached the blanket from over the shelter opening and rolled it up. Aimee had searched the inside of the shelter to make sure they weren't leaving anything. "Got everything?" he asked, looking around.

"I think so. What was that motor?"

"It was Kinnard on his snowmobile. He just took off on it." Matt took her arm. "Aimee, as far as I can tell, right now William is in there alone with a young woman who appears to be taking very good care of him."

"Really?" Her breath hitched. She squinted toward the cabin. "You saw him? He's all right? Can I see? Oh, Matt. Can we go now?"

"Listen to me. We've got to act fast." Her gaze was still on the cabin. He grabbed her shoulder. "Aimee, look at me. Concentrate. William is safe. I need you to pay attention. You have to do exactly as I say. Kinnard headed north. He may be planning to hide up there and watch for us."

Matt rubbed his thumb across his lower lip and looked up at the sky. "The snow is coming down harder, so that's on our side. If we circle around to the south side of the cabin, and the snow keeps up, we should be able to sneak inside without him seeing us."

"What about the girl? Won't she see us?"

"When I saw her, she didn't act as if she were being watched. There didn't appear to be anyone else there, either. She was totally concentrated on the baby. But we have to go in as if there are armed guards in every room."

He set his jaw and looked Aimee straight in the eye. "That means you can't go rushing to William. You have to be strong. You must stay with me and do exactly as I say." He gripped her arms. "Can you do that?"

Her eyes glittered with dampness. She opened her mouth but nothing came out.

"Can you?" he growled. "Because if you can't, you're going to have to stay up here, hidden, until I can get him. I can't take care of both of you at once."

CHAPTER 10

AIMEE CLOSED her eyes and took a deep breath. Then she lifted her chin. "I can do it."

He pushed away his need to touch her, to pull her close and kiss her and promise her everything was going to be all right. This was a mission—he needed to act like a commander. Somewhere inside himself, he had to find the detachment and focus that made him good at his job.

And Aimee had to act like a soldier. "This is a covert operation, Aimee. I'm the commander, and you're my team. You follow my orders. If I say abort—then we abort the mission and retreat. Is that understood?"

Her lower lip trembled visibly, and her eyes glittered with unshed tears. But she nodded.

"Are you sure? Because if I give the order, you

have to leave William and do what I tell you. Can you do that?"

Her chin lifted. "Yes, sir."

Fierce longing and aching compassion took his breath away. For one instant, he abandoned his Special Forces training and allowed himself to be just a man. He cupped her cheek and leaned in to kiss her trembling lips. When their lips touched, a thrill swirled through him that nearly buckled his knees. "I swear to God, Aimee, if you can trust me, I will save your baby."

She pulled away and gave him a solemn look. "I trust you," she whispered.

It took forty minutes to trudge down the hill and around to the south side of the cabin. Despite what Matt had told Aimee, he was hampered by her. If he'd thought for a minute he could have safely left her in the shelter while he rescued William, he'd have done it.

If he thought he could wait until he could get a message through to Deke to fly a man in to help him, he'd have done that. But he had no time, and more importantly, no intention of leaving Aimee to fend for herself for even a short while. His mission was to protect both her and her baby, so he clenched his jaw and moved at a pace far slower than he wanted to. As they approached the southern downhill side of the cabin, he quickly repeated his instructions to Aimee.

"I'll go in first. You wait for my hand signal. I'll wave you on as soon as I can verify that the room is clear. If you don't see me, you stay right where you are until you do." He looked at her evenly. "What do you do if I don't come back out?"

She swallowed. "After ten minutes, I head for the door and—and give myself up." She paused. "Matt—?"

"No. No questions. You give yourself up."

She nodded reluctantly.

"Okay, once we're inside—do you remember what I told you about the layout?" He was going by what he remembered from his early teens. He hoped to hell he was at least partly right.

"The big room is in front," she said. "The right-hand door goes to a bedroom, the left-hand door goes to the kitchen."

"Correct, and the kitchen is where I saw the girl holding William."

"You're going through the bedroom and around to the kitchen from the north side. You'll wait until I go in through the south door and surprise her. When you hear me speak, you'll come through the north door."

She nodded.

"Good. After that, just listen to me. I'll tell you what to do."

He looked at her and sent her what he hoped was an encouraging smile. "Ready?"

AIMEE'S THROAT CLOSED UP, but she nodded. A week ago, if anyone had told her she'd be part of a mountain rescue mission to save her own son, she'd have called them insane. Now, here she was, ready to stage a dangerous rescue at the side of a special ops soldier and one of the best search and rescue specialists in the country. They were about to rescue her seven-month-old son from kidnappers.

A trembling started deep within her and quickly spread out to her hands, arms, and knees. She held onto the Glock with both hands, hoping it would give her strength and courage.

In front of her, Matt stole forward, his entire body tense with expectation. He was ready for anything. His broad shoulders looked strong enough to support the world. His body, even in the bulky coat and camo pants, moved with the powerful grace of a big cat—a leopard maybe, or a cougar.

Her insides clenched in desire as she remembered the silky roughness of his stubbled cheek and chin contrasting with the firmness of his lips. The power of his body against her, his chest and belly rising and falling with his rapid breaths, then the feel of his rigid shaft pushing into her, filling her with molten longing. He was so strong, yet he could be so gentle. She knew if anyone in the world could save her baby, Matt could.

He turned his head and glanced at her over his shoulder, his profile strong and assured as a warrior. Then he gestured, waving her forward and pointing to an evergreen tree.

She rose to an uncomfortable crouch and eased forward, staying in the shadow of the tree. Her pulse sped up and her mouth went dry.

Matt shifted his weight to the balls of his feet, then held up his hand, thumb and first finger forming an *O* for Okay. She sent him the same gesture back. He gestured to her that he was about to move forward.

He'd given her the five-minute crash course in signals so she knew what he was telling her. He didn't look back at her so her responding nod was wasted. As he half-crawled, half-crept toward the two steps that led to the cabin's door, she waited. Her limbs twitched with the need to move.

She fought to keep her breathing even as she watched him unlock the door and slip inside. He'd warned her that once he disappeared into the house, she'd feel an almost uncontrollable urge to follow him. *It's the hardest thing to learn about stealth reconnaissance,* he'd explained. *When your commander gives you an order, his life and yours rest on him being able to trust you to carry out that order, even if all it means is that you stay still.*

She'd understood, or so she'd thought. But now she burned to move a few steps forward, enough to be able to see through a window. She set her teeth and clenched her fists. She would not move, no matter how much she ached to see her baby. Her scalp burned, and despite the cold air, a drop of sweat ran down her back. "Come on, Matt," she muttered. "Hurry up."

MATT STOOD AS STILL as a stone in the cabin's living room, listening. Getting into the house had been easy. Moving through the house without making a sound was harder. He heard water running, and a feminine voice talking in low, soothing tones. Then he heard a giggle and a splash. The young woman was giving William a bath. The excruciating tension in his shoulders and neck relaxed, sending a rush of relief through him all the way from his head to his feet. William was safe and happy.

He needed to reconnoiter the kitchen before he gestured Aimee in. He didn't want to leave her outside any longer than he had to, but he'd ordered her to treat this like a mission, and he had to do the same thing. It was dangerous to leave Aimee out there undefended, but that's how he would handle it if she was a BHSAR specialist. Except that if she were a specialist, she'd know how long to wait and when to move, even if she didn't get a signal.

Matt glided closer to the kitchen door and peered in past the hinges. Although the light given off by the oil lantern was dim and flickering, his narrow view caught the edge of the sink. He saw William's arms waving, and the girl's hand gliding a soapy washcloth over his pink, new skin. She laughed. She sounded young, maybe not far out of her teens. Hopefully that was a good sign. If she were young and enchanted by William, chances were she'd be easily manipulated into talking about Kinnard.

He angled his head until his gaze spotted the rear door to the kitchen. In the dimness it was impossible to tell if it was unlocked, but at least he'd remembered correctly. There were two doors to the kitchen. He retraced his steps across the room, thankful that the floorboards were solid, not creaky. He slipped through the front door and closed it. Then he gestured for Aimee.

Immediately, she rose and moved stealthily forward and up the steps. He let out the breath he'd been holding. Thank God she was all right. He'd only taken a few seconds to reconnoiter, but he knew all too well that it took only a few seconds to kill.

"They're in the kitchen," he whispered in her ear. "She's bathing William and he's happy. He's splashing water everywhere."

She swallowed and then nodded. "Bath time is his favorite time of day. He thinks it's funny to splash water on me—" her voice cracked.

"It's okay, Aimee. He's right there and he's safe. Now I'm going around through the bedroom. Give me sixty seconds to get into place and then step through the left door—that's the door to the kitchen. Get the drop on the girl and be careful."

She hadn't taken her eyes off the door. He understood why. Her baby was on the other side of it. "Aimee, look at me. Get the drop on her. You know what I mean?"

She nodded. "Hold the gun on her."

"With your finger next to the trigger. Ready to pull the trigger if necessary. Can you do that?"

"Y-yes."

"Don't take your eyes off her for an instant and —" Her gaze had drifted back to the door. He touched her chin. "Look at me. "You can *not* let yourself get distracted by seeing William. This may be the most important thing you will ever do. Your life and your baby's depend on you being a soldier, not a mother. Our mission—your mission—is to rescue him. Do you understand?"

Pain lit her eyes and she took a breath to speak, then stopped and nodded.

"By the time you get the drop on her, I'll be coming in the rear door and we'll have her in our crossfire. Okay?"

"How do I know when sixty seconds has passed?"

He counted for her. "Count like that. Don't let your anxiety speed up the count."

She nodded. "Okay."

"One final thing. Get her to sit down. You keep away from the window. I saw her. That means Kinnard might be able to see you. Let's go." He peered around the door and then pushed it open. He gestured for her to go to the left door and he'd go to the right.

He pointed at his watch, indicating that she should start counting, then he slipped through the door and took a couple of precious seconds to study the bedroom. He'd give just about anything to find something that identified Kinnard's first name or any information about him or the girl. The most remarkable thing about the room was the quilt on the floor. He crossed to the bathroom, which led from the bedroom onto the enclosed back porch. Good. He'd remembered the layout.

The porch had a half-paned door and two windows. Directly in front of the back door was the door to the kitchen. Through it he could hear the girl talking to William but he couldn't make out what she said.

Come on, Aimee. He looked at his watch and saw that she had twenty more seconds. He itched to get in, grab the baby, and handcuff the girl before she knew what hit her. But he needed Aimee there to take her baby. Aimee needed her baby.

So he waited and watched the second hand crawl around.

FIFTY-NINE, sixty. Aimee took a deep breath, trying to control her anxiety. She adjusted her two-handed grip on the Glock, laid her shoulder against the door, and took a deep breath.

"Here we go, pretty boy—" the girl said. William gurgled happily.

Aimee's throat spasmed and her heart squeezed so tightly it hurt. *William.* She almost cried out loud. Closing her eyes for a second, she drew in another deep breath, and shouldered the door open, leading with her weapon. "Don't move!"

The girl shrieked and clasped William to her chest. "What? Who—?" She stepped backwards.

"I said—don't move." Aimee's nervousness was completely overshadowed by the horror of what she was doing. She swallowed against the bile that rose in the back of her throat. She'd never aimed a weapon at anyone in her life. Yet here she was, threatening a pretty young woman who was holding the baby she—Aimee—had given birth to. She was aiming a loaded gun in the direction of William, her own son. The thought and the action made her physically ill. She looked at the door behind them, absently noticing a pair of snowshoes hanging on a hook.

Where was Matt?

The woman had calmed down enough to shift William to her other arm. "Who are you?" she asked. "Where did you come from?"

"I'm asking the questions," Aimee snapped. "What's your name?" In the flickering lantern light, she could see that the young woman's hair was a flat beige color, and her shocked dark eyes were rimmed with pale lashes, which made her look younger than she probably was.

The young woman didn't answer.

"I asked you what your name is."

"Maddie," she said, her voice rising in pitch. She hugged William tighter, making Aimee's heart ache. "It's M-Maddie. What's going on? Who are you?"

Aimee gestured with the barrel of the pistol. "Sit down, Maddie."

As Maddie started around the table, William whimpered quietly. Aimee almost dropped the gun, but Matt's voice echoed in her ears. *Your life and your baby's depend on you being a soldier, not a mother.*

"No! Sit here." Aimee glanced at the window over the sink, where tie-back curtains hung. She needed them closed.

"Wait!" she shouted.

Maddie froze.

"Close the curtains." She gestured with the gun.

Watching Aimee warily, Maddie tucked William into the curve of one arm and reached for the curtain ties with the other. As soon as the fabric fell into place, obscuring the window, Aimee gestured again.

"Now sit."

Maddie obeyed. She bounced William on her lap.

Aimee's sore heart filled to bursting with equal amounts of joy and pain. Joy because her baby was obviously safe and happy. But the pain of watching her baby and not being able to hold him, to speak to him, was wrenching. She shivered. The kitchen was much warmer than outside, but she could feel a chilly breeze. "Why aren't you using that generator?"

Maddie looked from the baby to her and back again. "I had it on earlier. We're low on fuel."

Aimee glanced at the door to the porch. What was Matt doing? Why hadn't he burst through the door? She needed William. She needed to hold him as much as she needed her next breath, but she couldn't. She'd promised Matt she'd act like a soldier. He'd given her an order, and he expected her to carry it out. She couldn't be William's mother until Matt came in.

She quickly glanced around the kitchen, squinting in the dimness. Near the cabinets on the other side of the stove was a step stool. She lowered her head and crept across in front of the window, then nudged the stool closer to the kitchen table and sat on it. Her hands were getting tired, so she set the gun on her lap and rested one hand on the grip. The barrel was still aimed at Maddie.

Matt hadn't told her to talk to the girl, but he hadn't told her not to either. "Who hired you?" she demanded, her gaze still hungrily assessing every inch of her son's body, to make sure he was all right. Every time she spoke, his big blue eyes turned her way. It was the hardest thing she'd ever done not to look at him. If he started crying or even whimpered again, she didn't know if she could stop herself from picking him up.

"Hired me? I don't—"

"Don't lie to me." She picked up the Glock and aimed it at the girl's head. "Who brought you up here and left you to take care of—" Aimee paused. "What's the baby's name?" She didn't want Maddie to know the baby was hers. If the woman knew that, it would give her a weapon that Aimee couldn't counter.

Maddie licked her lips nervously and lifted

William to her shoulder. She patted his back. "I don't know his name. My boyfriend brought me up here. Listen, please don't hurt the baby."

Aimee couldn't stop herself from watching Maddie's hand comforting her baby. With a huge effort, she turned her attention back to Maddie and uttered a short, ironic laugh. "Don't hurt the baby? Oh, don't worry, Maddie, I'm not going to hurt the baby. But if you don't give me some straight answers, I am definitely going to hurt you."

"Okay, okay." Maddie licked her lips again. "My —my boyfriend told me he needed me to watch his —his niece's little boy for a few days. She's sick, and—"

"I said, the truth!"

"But that is   "

"You expect me to believe you're up here on the top of a mountain in a snowstorm because your boyfriend's niece has a cold?"

William's big bright eyes widened. He turned his head to look at her and frowned and began to whine.

Maddie's eyes grew wide and filled with tears. She sniffed. "You don't understand. When Chris tells you to do something, you don't get in his face about it, you know? I mean, he's been real good to me and all, but when he says do something, you just gotta do it." She shrugged and took her hand off William's back to wipe her nose on the sleeve of her sweater. William whined again and strained against Maddie's hold.

Aimee drew in a breath and gritted her teeth. "Who's Chris?"

"He's my boyfriend. I told you."

"Chris who?"

Maddie's eyes narrowed, as if she were weighing the advisability of telling a stranger Chris's full name. Then her gaze dropped to the Glock and she swallowed. "Chris Kinnard. Look, did he do something wrong? 'Cause I don't know nothing about it if he did. I just watch the baby."

Aimee lowered the gun again. It sounded like Maddie was completely in the dark about Chris's activities. But there was a slim chance that she was acting. Aimee's instincts told her to believe Maddie was telling the truth, but she couldn't trust her instincts. Those same instincts were screaming at her that her baby was whining because he knew her voice and he needed her.

His whining got louder and he squirmed in Maddie's arms. "He's tired," Maddie said softly. "I should put him down."

Fierce longing arrowed through Aimee. She tamped it down. "Where does he sleep?" She kept her voice as hard as she could make it.

"In—in the bedroom. I put a quilt on the floor."

"That's smart. You have children of your own?"

Maddie shook her head. "No, but I practically

raised my two little brothers. I know all about babies."

Aimee wondered why Matt was taking so long, but she knew there must be a reason. What if something had happened? He'd told her to give herself up if he didn't show. That was not going to happen. She was here, in a warm, safe house with only a skinny girl standing between her and her baby. Right now she was in charge. She had the advantage, and she had to keep it.

"Let's go. Take him into the bedroom." Aimee aimed the gun at Maddie again.

Maddie stood carefully, still patting William on the back. She started toward Aimee, toward the closed door where Matt was supposed to be.

"No!" Aimee snapped. "The other way." She stood and blocked the door.

Maddie looked surprised, but she turned and stepped through the doorway into the big front room and across to the bedroom door.

Aimee was right behind her.

Maddie shifted William and reached for an oil lamp.

"No light." Aimee took a deep breath. "You do what I tell you to, nothing more," she ordered the girl. "I don't want any lights turned on. Just put Wi —the baby—down."

"I need to diaper him," Maddie said.

"Do it." It broke Aimee's heart to watch another

woman do the things she always did for William. Her heart twisted in agony to have him so close, and yet too far, in every sense of the word, for her to touch.

Maddie quickly diapered William and put him in a warm sleeper. "There you go, darlin'," Maddie cooed. "Sleep tight." She leaned over and kissed William's round pink cheek.

Aimee nearly lost it. She bit her lip—hard—to stop herself from moaning aloud. "Sit down on the floor and keep your hands in your lap so I can see them."

Now William was crying and reaching out his little arms toward her. Aimee could tell how tired he was by the sound of his cries. She did her best to ignore him, but if Maddie didn't already know that she was William's mother, she'd figure it out any second.

She had to stay focused. *Had to.* She sat on the bed, leaned back against the headboard, and rested the gun hand on her lap. "Now, how about telling me who Chris is and who he works for."

MATT PRESSED his back against the wall next to the half-paned door, his MAC-10 in hand. He'd been about to burst in on Aimee and the girl when the clouds had parted, allowing the moon to light the snow-covered landscape.

Aware that Kinnard was still out there, probably waiting for a chance to ambush him, he'd flattened himself against the wall and carefully surveyed the clearing around the cabin. He wasn't worried about Aimee. He had listened to her barking orders and questioning William's caretaker. His chest had swelled with pride. She was handling the younger woman like a pro.

He was relieved when Aimee directed the young woman to take the baby into the bedroom. He would have much more freedom to handle Kinnard, knowing Aimee and William were out of the way.

Just as he'd decided it was safe to move across the porch to the kitchen door, he detected movement out of the corner of his eye. He angled slightly, just enough to check the area close to the house. Nothing. Maybe he'd seen a rabbit or a deer, or even a wolf, but he didn't think so. His instincts, honed by four years in Air Force Special Forces, told him it was a human predator. Crouching down, he crept across the porch to the door. He was taking a chance. If Kinnard saw the lantern's light, he'd know someone had opened the door.

But Matt would rather lure Kinnard to the kitchen than take a chance on him circling around to the front door. He wasn't about to be maneuvered into a position where Aimee and William were between Kinnard and him.

Matt slipped into the kitchen. The lantern was still lit, although it looked low on oil. The curtains were closed, but he knew his silhouette would be visible if he stood. He slinked across the wooden floor to the table and extinguished the lamp.

He pulled his infrared glasses down from his forehead. He figured Kinnard was likely to have infrared glasses too, so he stayed hidden as much as possible while he slipped back over to the porch door and opened it. Staying in the shadow of the open door, he rose enough to peer out. Sure enough, he spotted Kinnard sneaking down toward the house from the north. He recognized the man's burly silhouette. Kinnard's weapon was slung over his shoulder as he carefully picked his way across the snow from tree to tree.

Matt waited, watching. Once Kinnard got to the clearing, he'd have to step into the open to come any closer. Matt's fingers tightened on the MAC-10. He could take Kinnard out at any time. He'd used deadly force a few times as an Air Force special op, but always as a last resort. A *dead* last resort.

He wanted Kinnard alive. He wanted to find out who had hired the man and why. He knew he was capable of extracting every bit of information Kinnard had, if he were willing to apply the necessary impetus. Unwilling but prepared to kill Kinnard if necessary, he kept a bead on the man as he paused at the edge of the trees. As Matt watched, the kidnapper pulled on a pair of infrared glasses, swung his rifle off his shoulder, and held it ready as he stepped into the clearing.

As if on cue, clouds covered the moon. Without the glasses, Matt would be blind in the cloudy darkness. He could see Kinnard's heat silhouette, and he tracked him across the snow-covered ground through his gun's scope. Kinnard swung his rifle slowly across the windows and doors of the cabin. Matt ducked back into the shadow of the doorway as Kinnard swiveled the barrel his way.

He waited, counting the seconds, considering what he would do if he were the other man. After enough time had passed that Kinnard should have moved on to survey the next window, Matt took a chance and peered out. As he'd suspected, Kinnard was aiming at the far west window as he eased forward, his shadow crawling across the moonlit snow. Matt took a deep breath and rapidly crossed the door's opening, flattening his back against the left facing. Now he was in a better position to shoot if necessary.

He angled around the facing to get a better look at Kinnard's position. As he did, a shot rang out from nowhere near Kinnard, cracking the cold silent air. Kinnard dropped to the ground.

CHAPTER 11

AIMEE SHOT STRAIGHT UP off the bed at the sound of the gunshot. Before her brain could process what she'd heard, several other shots followed, each one quieter than the last. Echoes, she realized. But echoes of what? Matt's gun? Or Kinnard's rifle? Matt's gun was fully automatic, but she'd only heard the one shot and some echoes. That scared her—a lot. Had Matt been shot?

William had settled down a little, and Aimee knew it was a combination of his tiredness and the quiet darkness. But the noise roused him and he started crying again. Maddie reached for him.

"Stop!" Aimee barked, pointing the barrel of the Glock at Maddie's head. Maddie froze, her hands out, fingers spread.

"Don't move a muscle," Aimee whispered.

"That was a gunshot. It scared him," Maddie protested.

"Hush!" Aimee dared a quick glance at her baby. There wasn't another shot. What she heard was much more frightening. It was a low, deep rumbling that was impossible to pinpoint, but immediately recognizable. It was an avalanche.

"Avalanche," Maddie whispered, echoing Aimee's thought. Her fingers twitched, and her eyes darted back and forth from the gun in Aimee's hand to the baby.

Aimee stood and moved away from her, toward the door that led into the living room. She didn't want to take a chance that Maddie would try to rush her and take her gun away. "A small one, right?" Aimee asked. Living in Wyoming, Aimee knew about avalanches, but she'd never been in one.

Maddie's dark eyes met hers and she nodded. "Maybe, or just the beginning of one. That gunshot may have dislodged the wet snow."

Panic fluttered in Aimee's throat. She may have never been in an avalanche, but she'd heard the tragic news stories all her life. "Is it coming this way? What happens if it hits the cabin?"

Maddie shrugged. "This late in the year, when the weather's getting warmer, slides happen a lot. Can I pick up the baby? He's so scared."

Aimee looked at her son, then back at Maddie.

No, she wanted to say. *He's my baby. I'll pick him up.* But the only thing she knew about this woman was that she cared for William. She wouldn't hurt him. What she might do to Aimee if she let down her guard, Aimee didn't know.

Doing her best to keep her face expressionless, Aimee nodded. "Have you got a car seat?"

Maddie nodded. "Right there in the corner."

"Don't move. I'll get it." Aimee backed toward the corner and grabbed it. She sat it on the floor near Maddie, then backed away.

"Put him in it."

"Uh, you're his mother, aren't you?"

Aimee froze. Was she that transparent? "Why would you say that?"

Maddie smiled as she strapped William safely into his seat. "Like I told you, I took care of my baby brothers. He's so tired he can barely keep his eyes open, but he strains toward you every time you speak. And you can't keep your eyes off him. I don't know what Chris's doing, but I do know this baby needs his mama." She pushed the seat toward Aimee. "Take him. I know you're dying to."

Aimee felt her eyes filling with tears. "No. I can't." She'd promised Matt that she would be a good soldier. William was safe. She didn't have to hold him to know that. Her hands tightened on the Glock's handle and she shook her head. "He knows I'm here. And I know you've taken good care of him." William reached up his little arms and whimpered. He blinked several times and sniffled. Aimee grimaced as her body ached with the need to hold him. He was almost asleep.

"I've been waiting for someone to get here," Maddie said. "I called the police this morning, before Chris got here." Tears formed in her eyes and slipped down her face. "I know you don't trust me, but I really did take care of him."

"You made the anonymous call?"

"Please don't tell Chris. He gets mad. But I was afraid something would happen to the baby."

"Thank you, Maddie," Aimee said, just as another deep rumble filled the air and she felt a shudder. She had no idea if it were the cabin floor or her own legs shaking, until she saw the lantern's flame waver. She gripped the Glock tightly. First the gunshot and now an avalanche. Her head spun with panic and worry. Matt was out there. What if he'd been shot?

Had she found her baby only to lose Matt?

KINNARD HADN'T MOVED since he'd gone down. After a swift survey of the surrounding area, in case he could spot the shooter, Matt kept the MAC and his eye trained on the kidnapper's torso. He couldn't tell if any of the shadows he saw were blood, but he couldn't risk going out to check because the gunshot hadn't been from a Glock semiautomatic, or any other kind of hand gun. That shot had come from a rifle at least as powerful as the one Kinnard carried. A gun he'd heard firing before, when the kidnapper and Al Hamir had been firing at each other. It had to be Al Hamir, Novus Ordo's man, who'd followed Matt back from Mahjidastan.

Kinnard had shot Al Hamir at the ransom drop point. Matt had seen that blood. Now he knew for certain that Al Hamir's injury wasn't serious. It certainly hadn't kept him from following them. Al Hamir was trying to kill Kinnard. Matt assumed it was because Kinnard was trying to kill Matt. It would suit him if Kinnard and Al Hamir got into a crossfire, leaving Matt free to move Aimee and William to safety. It would be dangerous to let down his guard, though, so he crept back through the kitchen and into the front room. He was pretty sure Al Hamir's gunshot had come from the downhill side of the cabin. He wanted to try to pinpoint his location.

Just as he started across the floor, he heard Aimee's voice, ordering the girl to precede her out of the bedroom.

As soon as he saw her, he spoke quietly. "Aimee."

Both women jumped.

"Matt! Are you okay?"

"Yeah. Shh. Get down, both of you."

"Where did that shot come from?"

"South. Below the cabin. I think Kinnard took a bullet."

"Chris?" the young woman cried. "Chris is shot? Oh my God!" She set the car seat down on the living room floor. One hand went to her mouth and the other pressed against her stomach.

"Calm down, Maddie," Aimee snapped at her. "Don't move."

Matt pushed his infrared glasses up onto his forehead and watched the two women's silhouettes. "Is William okay?" he asked.

"He's fine. Maddie took very good care of him. Matt, she's the one who called in the tip."

"What? She called the police—?"

"Where is he? Where's Chris?" Maddie sobbed. "Is he in the kitchen?"

"He's outside," Matt said. "Settle down. We'll check on him as soon as I can be sure Al—the shooter—is gone."

"I have to check on Chris!" Maddie moved toward the front door.

"Maddie, wait!" Aimee cried.

"Stop!" Matt said. "I need to ask you some questions about the kidnapping."

Maddie stopped, but her hands flew to her

mouth. "No! How could you shoot him?" She broke for the door.

Matt dove for her, but she got to the door first and slipped through, pulling it closed enough to block Matt and slow him down.

"Matt, stop her! She'll get killed." Aimee headed for the door.

"Aimee, no!" He stepped in front of her and caught her against his chest. "Get down! Get William."

Aimee immediately dropped to her knees and crawled back to the baby.

"Stay here. That is an order." Matt slid through the open door and onto the front porch. Falling to his stomach, he held the MAC-10 ready to fire. He couldn't see anything.

He crept to the side of the porch, watching every direction. He didn't want to end up shot or captured. He still had work to do. He had to get Aimee and her baby off the mountain.

Maddie's voice sounded muffled and far away as she screamed for Chris. Matt needed to see around the side of the cabin, but the porch didn't extend to the corner. He pulled his infrared glasses over his eyes and scanned the area to the south, but he saw nothing that looked like a human. Sliding off the porch, he crawled westward along the cabin's wall, staying as much in the shadows as he could, keeping an eye out to the south for Al Hamir.

By the time he reached the southwest corner of the cabin, he could hear Maddie crying. Flattening himself against the cabin's wall, he peered around the corner and saw her crouched beside Kinnard, who was stirring. He breathed a sigh of relief. Maddie was okay, and Kinnard was still alive. He needed to question them both.

While he watched, Kinnard sat up with Maddie's help. Matt saw a patch of black on the front of his winter camos. Blood. He must have taken a bullet in his shoulder because he was moving pretty well. If he'd been hit in the chest, he wouldn't be upright.

Maddie rose to her knees, still holding onto Chris. A tiny red dot appeared on the side of her head.

"Look out!" Matt yelled, breaking into a run. He risked a glance behind him, but didn't see anything. He pushed his legs to pump as fast as possible through the wet snow. "Get down!" He was about four feet away from the two when Maddie turned her head in his direction. The red dot was centered on her forehead.

"Down!" Matt shouted. "Look out!"

Kinnard tried to pull her to the ground.

A loud crack drowned out all other sound.

Maddie's head jerked, then slowly, she toppled over.

"Maddie! Oh God!" Kinnard yelled, trying to get to his feet.

Matt saw the red dot slithering up Kinnard's chest and neck.

"Kinnard, duck!"

The kidnapper hit the ground and rolled sideways.

A second crack. Snow puffed as the bullet ploughed into the ground barely two inches from Kinnard's shoulder.

Matt dove into the snow and immediately rose up to shoot, but he knew his MAC wasn't powerful enough to reach the terrorist. He hurled himself across the snow-covered ground and grabbed for Kinnard's rifle, but the sling was twisted around the other man's arm.

A third shot zinged past Matt's head. At the same time, Kinnard rolled again and sat up, trying to untangle the rifle sling. After a couple of seconds, he got it loose and raised the weapon to his uninjured shoulder.

"You son of a bitch, your man shot Maddie!" Kinnard yelled.

"Not my man," Matt said. "You don't know him?"

"Hell no. Who the bloody hell is he?" Kinnard bellowed.

"Tell me who hired you, and I'll get you to the cabin."

"Go to hell." Kinnard brandished the rifle in Matt's direction, but Matt grabbed the barrel and twisted it sideways, then shoved the end of it into the snow.

"Listen to me. Do you know who hired you?" Matt growled, aiming the MAC-10 at him. "Was it Margo Vick?"

Kinnard let go of the rife with a groan. "All I know is I was told where the Vick's house was, what time to get there, and how to turn off the alarm."

Another shot rang out and Matt and Kinnard both dove for the ground. "You had to know who you were dealing with. You made the ransom call."

"No! I grabbed the kid and brought Maddie and him up here. The same guy who hired me told me to meet you for the ransom. He told me to kill the woman and the baby once I'd captured you. But Maddie wanted the baby—" he stopped. "Maddie!" he shouted, anguished.

Just then a low rumbling that Matt hadn't noticed grew louder. He felt the ground beneath them tremble. "Snow slide!" he shouted, scrambling to get his feet under him. He had to get to the cabin. Kinnard cursed and began crawling toward the trees.

The rumbling grew in volume. Matt looked to

the north, toward the peak of the mountain, and saw the white cloud foaming upward toward the heavens, obscuring the moon's light. He was at least forty feet from the cabin. There was no way he could make it. His only hope of survival was to find a tree and hold on for dear life. About eight feet uphill was a sturdy-looking evergreen. He lunged forward, scrambling to get a foothold in the wet snow. He managed to shove his way through the branches and wrap his arms around the trunk as the first billowing drifts of snow reached him. He ducked his head and locked his hands around the barrel of the MAC-10, praying that the tree and his fingers would hold. He was pretty sure he was going to be buried anyway. He changed his prayer. *Keep Aimee and William safe. Let Deke find them.*

AIMEE HEARD the roar and felt the ground shake. *Avalanche.* Muffled thuds jarred the walls and windows, rattling the glass. Snow, slamming into the cabin's walls.

"William!" she cried, throwing herself across the hardwood floor and grabbing his seat in her arms. A vague memory from childhood tickled the edge of her brain. A children's education piece on what to do in a snow slide. The most important thing, she recalled, was to keep a pocket of air in front of one's face, and of course, not to panic. She and William were inside, and probably safe, even if the cabin was buried, but what about Matt? He was out there with no protection.

She heard his voice as clearly as if he were next to her. *Take care of William. I'll take care of myself.*

You'd better, she answered silently. Holding onto William's car seat, she crawled across the floor to the central wall that divided the kitchen from the bedroom. It seemed like it would be the strongest place to wait out the slide. Unless the snow was heavy enough to crush the cabin, they might survive. She lay down against the wall and cradled William's seat against the curve of her body.

"Hi, William Matthew Vick," she whispered, touching his precious, soft, silky cheek for the first time since he'd been kidnapped. "Smile for me," she coaxed. He waved his arms and cooed.

She leaned forward to kiss his little face. "I know. I've been waiting a long time to see you, too." Her eyes filled with tears. She blinked and one fell on William's forehead. She wiped it away.

"Hang in there with me," she said softly. "I've got someone I want you to meet. He's a brave man. He took care of your daddy and he took care of me."

As she spoke the words, she realized she meant them. Matt would have done everything in his power to save Will—even sacrificed himself if it meant Will could have lived to see his son. That was the kind of man Matt was. She smiled sadly and blinked away her tears. "A very brave man," she whispered as the rumbling of the cascading snow grew louder and the cabin's timbers creaked and groaned. Behind her, glass shattered. She pulled William closer and covered his seat with her torso and arms.

AS THE SNOW piled up around Matt, he worked to propel himself upward by reaching for higher and higher branches. He knew he was very near the top of the slide, so as long as he could hold on and stay as close to the top of the snow as possible, he could ride it out. But his arm muscles stung and cramped with exertion, and he wasn't going to be able to hold on much longer. One of the newer theories of surviving a snow slide was the granular convection—or Brazil Nut—effect. The theory was that when shaken, larger particles rose to the top of water, snow, or in the case of Brazil nuts, a can of mixed nuts. The idea was to let the moving snow shake you to the top as smaller rocks and limbs were plowed under. Many experts felt it made more sense than trying to swim in the snow by flailing one's arms.

The snow was piling up near his head, and his arms and legs were trembling they were so tired.

The tree's trunk was bent almost double and its roots were coming loose from the ground.

Matt figured if the Brazil nut theory was wrong, he had two chances—slim and none. But he opted for optimism. With a deep breath and gripping the MAC-10 as tightly as he could with his frozen right hand, he let go of the tree and let the snow carry him down the mountain.

Take care of William, he whispered silently to Aimee. *Don't worry about me.* As the snow billowed around him and he covered his nose and mouth with his left arm, warm tears mixed with snow crystalized on his cheeks.

MATT WAS AFRAID TO MOVE, afraid of finding out that he couldn't. For a few minutes, he lay doubled in on himself like a fetus, waiting for the courage to test his limbs, to see if they worked. He'd count himself lucky if his fingers and toes didn't break off when he finally decided to wiggle them.

The last thing he remembered was floating on snow in the darkness. He could tell that the air around him was getting warmer. But strangely, there was also warmth below him. Warmth and sticky wetness. *Don't let it be blood.*

Not yet ready to move, he assessed his position. His head, covered by his parka's hood, was tucked between his shoulders, and the coat's hem was pulled down as far as it would go over his butt. He didn't remember doing any of that. All he remembered was letting go of the tree and floating downhill on a wave of snow, all the while praying that Aimee and her baby were all right. *Aimee!*

He straightened—or he tried to. He couldn't move, and it wasn't just because his muscles were icy cold. Something was on top of his torso, weighing him down. Snow? He took a deep breath, preparing to push against the weight, and his nostrils filled with the unmistakable spicy smell of evergreen needles.

He tried to straighten his arms and legs, and pain shrieked along his nerve endings. Nausea engulfed him. Sternly, he forced his brain to rise above the pain and think rationally.

One part of his body hurt more than all the rest, but for the life of him he couldn't figure out which part it was. The pain seemed to be everywhere at once. And the nausea was making it worse. He stuck out his tongue and lapped at a few snowflakes that were caught on his lips. Their chill felt good in his mouth.

Carefully, he flexed his ankles, relieved that his brain still had that much control over his limbs, and waited. They weren't causing the nauseating pain. After a few agonizing seconds, his cold calf muscles responded and relaxed. Matt blew out a breath. One by one, he tested each muscle without actually moving. Each time, he cringed and braced himself for the shrieking pain. It was a slow, excruciating process. Finally, he concluded that his feet and legs weren't the problem.

Then he realized that, while he'd lifted his head, he hadn't opened his eyes. When he did, he saw the crisscrossed shadows of evergreen branches. The evergreen smell, mixed with the smell of wood and blood—. *Oh, hell.* The sticky stuff was blood. He looked down at himself, and saw where the blood had come from. A slender branch was sticking through his left forearm.

He gagged, and his mouth filled with acrid saliva as his stomach heaved. Icy sweat beaded on his face and trickled down the side of his neck. What if that wasn't the only branch that had impaled his body? What if he couldn't get to Aimee and William?

Lying still, Matt wracked his brain for a way to free himself from the tree. He had a small handsaw in his backpack. He groaned in frustration. The backpack had burned up in the Hummer. What did he have on him? A knife. In a scabbard attached to his belt. Now if he could just get to it.

In between several bouts of nausea and a couple of unmeasured periods of unconsciousness, he finally worked the knife out of its scabbard with his right hand. Afterward, he barely remembered

anything about the process, except for the awareness that he was taking much too long and not
thinking very clearly.

Once he had the knife in his hand, it was only a
matter of about half an hour of excruciatingly slow
and careful sawing to cut the thin branch loose
from the larger branch attached to the tree. It took
another thirty or forty minutes to extricate himself
from underneath the larger branch. All in all, it was
a miracle he lived through it. And a miracle that the
thin branch hadn't broken a bone. He shuddered,
hoping the miracles didn't run out too soon,
because he was pretty sure he was going to need a
few more of them.

As hard as he tried to pretend that it wasn't a
problem having his forearm skewered on a stick, he
knew better. So much for miracles. With only one
arm, he wasn't sure even a miracle could help him
save Aimee and William. But he had to try.

As he put his right glove back on, he heard
something. It was a baby—crying. William! He was
close. At least he was close to them. He sighed in
relief. Now all he had to do was figure out exactly
where he was in relation to Aimee and the baby.

Looking around, he noticed that whatever he
was sitting on, it was a few feet above the
surrounding snow. He blinked, trying to get his
bearings. Maybe if he stood. He tried to tuck his
left arm hand against his chest, but the stick was in

the way. It hit him in the chest and the pain almost knocked him out.

With a sick desolation, he faced the truth. He couldn't do anything until he got rid of the piece of wood. The good news was that it was barely more than a twig—maybe a half-inch in diameter, with about two inches sticking out of his arm on either side. The bad news was that the two inches that stuck out was hardly enough to grip. With his right hand, he picked up a twig lying nearby and put it between his teeth, then tried to view his impaled arm detachedly, as if it were someone else's. For a few minutes, he bathed his forearm in snow, numbing it with cold.

Then, biting on the twig, he carefully wrapped his right hand around the two inches of bloody wood protruding from the inside of his arm. He took deep breaths until he was drunk on oxygen. Then with a loud roar, he slowly and deliberately pulled the stick out of his arm.

And passed out.

CHAPTER 12

MATT'S ARM hurt like hell. He opened his eyes and looked at the matching holes on either side of his forearm where the stick had been. He frowned. Stick? Eventually, he remembered that his arm had been impaled on a small branch and that he'd pulled it out himself. Maybe it was a good thing that he didn't recall the specifics.

The two holes on his arm were oozing blood. Another miracle. The stick hadn't shredded an artery. If it had, he'd have probably bled to death and never woken up. He licked dry, chapped lips and tried to sit up. He examined the sky. There was a heavy cloud cover that was almost as dim as dusk. It could definitely portend another storm. After a quick glance around the landscape, he looked down. He was sitting on something metallic. He brushed snow away to reveal a slab of tin. A tin roof? He and the tree were on top of the cabin!

His whole body trembled in relief. That's why he'd heard William crying. Aimee and her baby were directly below him. All he had to do was get to a door or window. Then he could get them out and get them to the next rendezvous point and they'd be safe.

Rendezvous point. *Deke.*

Matt shook his head as trepidation churned in his stomach. How was he going to get them there? He wasn't even sure he could stand up. He'd arranged for Deke to put down at the coordinates at 0900 hours. But he didn't know if Deke had fixed the helicopter or what the weather conditions down the mountain were. He needed to talk to Deke. Awkwardly digging into the inside pocket of his parka with his right hand, he pulled out the satellite phone. He pressed the call button, not sure if he could get a signal through the cloud cover or not. The light came on. Thank God the battery wasn't frozen. He read the time on the phone's display. It was about ten minutes past eight. He punched in Deke's number.

"Matt!" Deke's voice was distorted by static. "Son of a gun! What the hell's going on?"

"Deke." His voice was hoarse and shaky. He cleared his throat. "Are we on for 0900?"

Static filled his ear. He turned his head, trying to get a better signal.

"—don't know if I can—put down—"

"Deke," Matt shouted. "0900. 0900. Be there."

"—firmative—"

He knew what Deke was worried about. He was afraid that the new snow would make it impossible for him to set the helicopter down near the peak, but he would be there. It was up to Matt to make sure Aimee and William got there. Between them, he and Deke would figure out how to get them into the helicopter.

Matt checked the battery life of his phone. Not good. It was down to one bar. Batteries lost power fast at below freezing. He pocketed it and awkwardly pushed himself to his feet, holding his throbbing left arm close against his chest. The first thing he saw was the barrel of the MAC-10, sticking out from under a dusting of snow and partially hidden by the tree. He grabbed it, wondering if the cold had rendered it useless. Then he scanned the landscape, assessing the slide's wreckage.

The slide had deposited what looked like about two feet of powder over the snow that had already fallen. About twenty yards away, something stuck up at an odd angle from of the snow. Matt squinted. It was clothed in winter camo. It was Kinnard. Damn. Based on the angle and rigidity of his body, he had to be dead and either frozen or in rigor.

Turning toward the south, he searched for any sign of Al Hamir, with no luck. His best estimate of where Al Hamir's rifle shots had come from put the terrorist beyond the worst of the piled-up snow. If he'd stayed put, he was probably unhurt. He couldn't afford to assume that Al Hamir was no longer a threat. He had to operate as though the terrorist had survived the slide. He surveyed the whole visible landscape, but didn't see any new footprints or any disturbance of the new snow. He saw no sign that suggested anyone had been there.

Kinnard might be dead, but Al Hamir was still alive. That meant Aimee was still in danger. Because although Novus needed Matt alive so he could be questioned, he had no use for Aimee or her baby.

Matt glanced back at Kinnard's frozen body and spotted the assault rifle, half-buried in the snow. He needed that rifle. He carefully walked over to the edge of the tin roof and let himself slide down the few feet to the ground. He forced himself through the snow to Kinnard's body. First, he confirmed that Kinnard was dead. Then he dug the rifle out with his good hand.

Turning back toward the cabin, he examined the tree that had fallen onto the cabin's roof, and onto him. Its roots were still partially embedded in the ground. And that meant that only part of the tree's weight was resting on the cabin.

At that instant, the tree creaked and settled, shaking the cabin. Its movement drew his attention to a large branch that had penetrated the roof as thoroughly as the stick had penetrated his arm. Fear screamed through him. *Don't let Aimee or William be hurt.*

Matt cautiously approached the downhill side of the cabin. As he got closer, he saw the damage the big tree had caused. The sides of the cabin had been crushed.

The slight bump he saw in the roof line told him the central portion of the structure had withstood the weight of the tree better than the sides, but the way the tree was creaking and moving, its roots might give way at any minute and its full weight would flatten the cabin. He had to get Aimee and her baby out of there.

Cradling his hand, he climbed over the snowdrifts and landed on the porch with a thud, jarring the hell out of his arm. The pain was like a punch to his gut. For a few seconds, he couldn't get his breath as dizzying nausea wracked him. Then he heard William crying again. He couldn't tell exactly where the sound was coming from, and ice crystals had formed on the panes of the door. He rubbed them away, trying to see inside.

"Aimee!" he called. "Aimee! Are you okay?" He

couldn't see anything through the glass panes. The inside of the cabin was pitch-dark.

"Aimee! Answer me!"

She didn't.

THE HEAVY TREE that lay on top of the cabin shifted as the snow melted around it, and the roof creaked and groaned. Aimee shook her head as she stared at the huge branch that had speared through the cabin's roof right in front of the wall where she'd huddled all night with William. It had missed them by several feet, but somehow that wasn't comforting.

She jumped and cringed as a thud reverberated through the cabin. Another tree falling? She wasn't sure. All she knew was that the loud bang was the latest in a long night full of very scary sounds, many of them from the cabin itself. The center wall where she'd huddled with William had turned out to be a very good choice. When the tree had hit the cabin, glass had popped out of windows and studs had cracked loudly. Nails screeching against wood, and logs crunching under the weight of the tree, had continued all through the night.

Every screech, every crunch had Aimee cringing and hovering over William to protect him, terrified that the cabin's structure wouldn't hold for another second.

She clutched William closer and whispered to him. "I know, William, I know. You're so uncomfortable. Your mommy isn't taking very good care of you." She took a shaky breath. "You're wet and hungry, and all I've got is this cold bottle of formula."

Earlier, she'd tried to breastfeed him, but stress and dehydration had left her with no milk. She'd dared to leave him long enough to weave her way into the kitchen around the debris. She'd found a bottle turned upside down on the drain board, with its top beside it. Further searching had yielded two cans of baby formula.

William had taken a little formula, but he scrunched up his face, making sure his mommy knew he didn't like it. That plus his reaction to her fear made him fussy.

She'd held him through the rest of the night, singing lullabies and trying to pretend for his sake that she didn't believe they were the only survivors of the snow slide. Trying to believe that Matt was out there somewhere, trying to get to them.

"Aimee!"

She stopped murmuring to William and listened. She'd dozed a few times during the night, only to wake up thinking she heard Matt calling her. But it always turned out to be the wind howling or the timbers of the house rubbing together.

"Matt?" It was foolish, she knew, to answer the wind, but there was nobody to hear her except William.

"Aimee? Are you all right? Answer me!"

The voice was gruff and hoarse, but it sounded real. She held her breath, listening. Hoping with every fiber of her being that it really was Matt while at the same time fearing she was hallucinating. She was desperately afraid that he hadn't survived. Then she heard a pounding on the door. She looked up. Pushing herself to her feet, still clutching William to her chest, she forced her stiff muscles to move.

She had to thread her way around the limb that had impaled the roof and duck fallen beams and avoid broken glass, but she finally got to the door. She rubbed frost off the glass. "Oh, Matt! It's really you."

"Aimee."

Standing in front of the door, surrounded by white snow, he looked like an angel. The parka's hood was pushed back. His ears were bright red, his cheeks were chapped, and his mouth was compressed into a thin grim line, but he was there. And he was beautiful. He grabbed the door knob and pushed. It didn't move.

"Matt, the cabin's crushed—"

"Get away from the door." She barely had enough time to back up before he put his right shoulder against it and shoved. Something cracked, and a broken board fell, barely missing his arm.

"Matt, stop! You're going to get hurt." Aimee had never seen him so desperate.

He kicked away the board and pulled his MAC-10. "Get as far back as you can. I'm going to break the window."

"Wait!" Aimee yelled as forcefully as she could.

He stopped, surprised.

"Matt, the door's stuck, and the cabin is collapsing. Slow down. We need to figure out what to do."

He pressed a gloved hand against the glass. "Listen to me. We don't have time. Deke is going to be at the peak in less than fifteen minutes. I've got to get you and William up there."

Her first reaction was excitement. "Deke's coming?" They were safe. But Matt's face told a different story. He looked exhausted, desperate, defeated. Shifting William's weight to her right arm, she laid her left hand against his right on the other side of the cold glass. "What's wrong?" she asked softly.

He laid his forehead against the glass. The corners of his mouth were white and pinched. "My phone is almost dead. I won't be able to contact Deke again."

Aimee heard what he didn't say. This was their

last chance. "Break the windows," she said, and backed away.

He met her gaze. She wasn't sure what he was looking for in her eyes, but she knew by looking at him that his goal was the same as hers. Get William to safety. He swung the handle of the MAC-10 at the panes of glass.

She wanted to cry at the weakness of his swing. He was exhausted. He'd spent the night out in the freezing cold. He'd fought to get to them. She was terribly afraid that he was using up the last dregs of his strength to save her baby. She was willing to let him do it.

Several blows later, there was a fair-sized hole in the door. Not large enough for her to easily get through, but plenty of room for the car seat.

"Matt, stop! That's enough." Without waiting to hear his response, she ran back to the wall and secured William into the car seat. Then she took one of the blankets she'd used for warmth and wrapped it around the seat.

When she looked up, Matt was bracing himself to swing again. "Get back," he shouted.

His hoarse voice and his pinched face attested to his exhaustion. He was hovering at the end of his strength. Would he make it to the peak? She had to believe he would.

"Matt. There's no time. Here."

"What are you doing?" Matt cried. "Another couple of minutes and—"

"No," she said flatly. "Take William and run. I'll climb out and follow."

He stared at her as if he didn't understand what she was saying. After a second, he nodded.

She kissed William and took a precious few seconds to whisper to him. "I swore once I got you back in my arms I'd never ever let you go. You're the most important thing in my life. You are my life. But I can't keep you safe here."

She touched his chin and he giggled, which brought tears to her eyes. "Matt's going to take you someplace where you'll be safe, and I'll see you soon, okay? You can trust him. I do."

She kissed him one last time, then wrapped another blanket around the car seat and handed it through the broken panes to Matt. When he reached out his right hand to take the seat's handles, Aimee saw the blood that stained the left sleeve of his parka.

"Matt, you're bleeding."

He shook his head. "Not so much anymore."

"Can you make it?"

His grim mouth flattened. The only color in his face was the bright spots on his cheeks. "I'll make it. You hurry," he rasped.

"I'm right behind you."

Gripping William's seat, he turned away.

"Matt—" Aimee called.

He looked over his shoulder at her.

"I trust you."

For an instant, his gaze held hers, then he nodded and turned. He carefully maneuvered the sloping hill of snow in front of the cabin, holding tightly to the car seat with his right hand.

Aimee looked at the hole in the door. The broken glass and wood surrounding it looked ominously sharp and dangerous. The baby had been protected by the double layer of blanket that covered him and by their careful maneuvering of the car seat through the space. She needed to knock out the shards of glass and splinters of wood so she could crawl through. She grabbed a slender stick of firewood and smashed as much of the glass as she could.

She eyed the hole. It looked pretty safe now. She dragged the quilt from the living room and padded the bottom of the hole, then put on her parka. She tossed her daypack and snowshoes out the hole and then remembered the pair she'd seen hanging in the kitchen. She tossed them out too, then hoisted herself through the hole and followed them, landing in the snow. As fast as she could, she fastened on her snowshoes and headed up the hill in the direction Matt had gone.

MATT HEARD the helicopter long before he saw it. The rhythmic drone of the propellers was strangely soothing. He matched his pace to the engine's cadence. At least he was warming up. Probably the combined efforts of climbing and maintaining his balance with only one arm.

Setting the baby seat on a downed tree trunk, he lifted the blanket slightly to check on William. It was the third time he'd peeked. No matter how much he lectured himself that he needed to keep the blanket in place so William didn't get cold, he found it impossible to go more than a few minutes without checking on him. William was fussy and unhappy, but he'd stopped crying. That worried Matt—like he knew anything about kids. He figured the baby was wet or hungry or both. He hoped that was all that was wrong. But as fussy as William was, whenever Matt checked him, his blue eyes latched onto Matt's and widened.

"Do you have any idea who I am?" Matt whispered. "I'm your godfather. Not that I deserve to be. I haven't done a very good job of taking care of you so far, but I'm hoping I can fix that in just a couple of minutes."

William waved his arms and whined.

"I know. It's cold. But you're about to have an adventure that possibly no man your age has experienced." His mouth twitched. "That's right," he said. "You are a man. A little man right now, but a man. A good man, like your daddy."

As he spoke, the sound of the helicopter got louder. The propellers appeared from the other side of the mountain, rising up like a dramatic scene in a war movie. Matt set the car seat down and waved with his right hand.

Deke was a welcome sight in his trademark sunglasses and his helmet and earpiece. He maneuvered the bird so that he was hovering almost directly over Matt's head. The downdraft created by the propellers whipped the snow around like a blizzard. It lofted a corner of the blanket that protected William. Matt knelt and tucked the corners more securely around the baby.

When he glanced up, Deke was holding up his satellite phone. Matt reached for his, hoping the battery hadn't died. To his relief, its light was on.

"I'm glad to see you're still upright. The weather service reported an avalanche, and I could see the results when I flew in." Deke's voice was cut by static.

"I rode it. Kinnard and his girl didn't make it."

"Damn. Where's Aimee? She and the baby okay?"

Matt nodded. "Aimee's on her way. I've got the baby here."

"Brock came along for the ride," Deke said. "I

can't land, and there's a storm almost here. They're showing lightning."

Matt knew that Deke couldn't risk the helicopter being damaged by lightning. "Just drop the basket," he yelled into the phone. "You're taking the baby."

A surprised expletive slipped from Deke's lips. Then he recovered. "You got it. Be right back." The helicopter rose and angled away from the mountain peak. Matt knew what he was doing. He needed room to hover while Brock readied the metal basket to be lowered on the wire rope.

While he waited, Matt made sure that William was snugly strapped in his safety seat. Then he tucked the blanket in tightly. "Okay, William Matthew Vick. You ready for your great adventure?" To his utter shock, William giggled. Matt couldn't stop himself from smiling. He pulled off his glove and traced the baby's plump cheek with his forefinger.

"You're as beautiful as your mother," he whispered, surprised when his voice broke.

Above him Deke was back, maneuvering until he hovered directly over them again, blasting them with downdraft. Matt couldn't see the heavy metal basket through the clouds of snow until it was almost on them. He grabbed the cold steel.

Even the slightest movement made his arm shriek with pain. But the only way he could hang onto the basket was to embrace the line with his left arm. By the time he picked up William's seat and lifted it over and in and secured the basket with bungee cords, he was dizzy and sick with pain. He looked up, barely able to make out Brock's form, He waved, sweeping his right arm as widely as he could, hoping Brock could see. Then he clung to the basket until he felt the wire rope start to stiffen. As he let go, the basket began to rise.

He watched, not breathing, as Brock stood at the edge of the helicopter door and guided the wire. When it was close enough, Brock leaned out and grabbed the basket, lifting it in through the open door. Once it was safely inside, Brock waved and Matt's satellite phone rang.

Matt answered.

"—the hell's wrong with your arm?"

"Forget it," Matt growled. "Get the baby out of here."

"Hey! There's Aimee."

Matt whirled. Aimee trudged toward them in snowshoes. She waved her arms. "It's Aimee!" he said.

"What about you two? Storm should be through here in about two hours. How about we say 1500 hours?"

"Affirmative," Matt replied. Matt had wracked his brain about where Deke could safely set the helicopter down. The planned tertiary rendezvous place was a clearing two miles southwest from the cabin. It was probably the best choice. "Tertiary rendezvous," he yelled into the phone.

Deke shook his head and shrugged. "Wha—?"

The static was growing. Matt knew his phone was about to go dead. "Ter—tiary ren—dez—vous," he enunciated slowly.

Deke ducked his head, listening. Then nodded. "—tiary—Rog—Out."

Relief nearly buckled Matt's knees. Deke had heard him.

Deke spoke, but all Matt got was static. He looked at his phone's display in time to see the battery light go out. It was dead. That was it. This was the last communication until they were rescued. If they were rescued. He waved the phone and shook his head.

But Deke was already turning the helicopter. As he took off, leaving more flying swirls of snow in his wake, Aimee walked up, breathing hard. She touched Matt's arm and said something, but Matt had no idea what.

He fell to his knees, his stomach heaving and clenching, although there was nothing in it. Then he raked up a small handful of snow and let it dissolve on his tongue, hoping the chill would chase away the queasy dizziness.

"Matt!" She knelt beside him.

The pain in his forearm was a constant agony,

made worse by the numbness in his fingers. He unzipped his parka and tucked his hand inside, hoping to warm his fingers without having to move them. He shivered.

He staggered to his feet. "I'm okay," he rasped.

"The hell you are!" she cried.

CHAPTER 13

Aimee got the snowshoes fastened over Matt's shoes and then guided him back down the hill toward the cabin. It was terrifying how weak and sick he was. Distinctive spots of red stained his cheeks, standing out like spotlights against his pale skin and pinched mouth. His left hand was tucked inside his unzipped parka, and blood stained the sleeve—more blood than before.

"We can't go in there," Matt muttered. "Tree might fall."

"I know. I'm just getting some supplies."

"Supplies? I'll do it." He bent down to unfasten the snowshoes and wavered, putting out a hand to steady himself.

"You stay back. I can do this."

He lowered his gaze and nodded. That sent an arrow of hurt through her. Not because she needed his help, but because he knew he was too weak to offer it.

Aimee tossed the daypack in through the hole in the door, then crawled in after it. Running into the kitchen, she carefully chose a few things. Too much and it would be too heavy to carry. She went through the kitchen drawers, looking for anything that might come in handy. One of the drawers was filled with first aid supplies. She knew there was nothing but gauze and strip bandages in the daypack, so she added antibiotic ointment, more gauze, tape, and a small bottle of alcohol. Then she saw a pair of scissors and stuck them in the pack as well.

Lifting the pack, she grimaced at its weight, but decided that she could handle it.

She lifted the daypack through the broken window and lowered it by one strap as far as she could before she let it fall to the ground. Then she climbed back through the hole.

Matt sat on a branch that stuck out from the fallen tree. He stood. His face was set, with lines of pain etching it. His eyes were too bright and appeared sunken, and his face was a horrible grayish color. She pasted a smile on, trying not to show how worried she was about him. "Okay," she said, trying to sound upbeat. "I've got everything. How far are we going?"

"About two miles."

"Two miles? That's not bad. Deke's going to meet us?"

He nodded. "At 1500 hours. Three o'clock."

She frowned. "Isn't that a long time?"

"Not really. About five hours from now. He needs time for the—sun to melt the snow," he said raggedly. "And we need time to get there. Let's go."

"No." Aimee crouched and unzipped the daypack. She dug in it for the first aid items. "I need to take care of your arm. You're still bleeding. What did you do?"

He caught her arm. "No."

"Matt, yes! You're about to collapse. You can't go any further until we stop that bleeding."

"Not here. The tree—"

As if on cue, the branches creaked and scraped across the tin roof. She had forgotten about the tree. Of course. They had to get out of the way, in case it fell. "Come on, then. Let's get away from here."

"Go on," Matt said tightly. "I'll follow."

"Oh no, you don't. You took care of me when I was hypothermic. It's my turn. Which direction?"

He checked his compass, then pointed. She slung the daypack onto her back, sticking her arms through the straps. "Will it help you to lean on me?"

Matt's mouth turned up in a wry smile. "I already am," he muttered. "More than I should."

After a couple of seconds, he shook his head. "No. Please go on. I'm going to be slower than—than you."

Aimee could tell his voice was getting weaker. *Don't quit on me,* she wanted to say. But that wasn't fair. He'd pushed himself farther than she ever would have been able to. He wasn't quitting. His wounded body was betraying him.

She headed south for about fifty feet and stopped at a fallen tree trunk that was about the right height for sitting. She brushed snow off and waited for him to catch up. He walked slowly, doggedly, as if all that was keeping him on his feet was determination. It broke her heart to watch his struggle. It took all her self-control not to run to help him. Her eyes burned and her throat closed, but she busied herself with unloading the first aid supplies.

When he got to her, she looked up, masking her feelings with a smile. "Sit down and let me see your arm."

He didn't even try to argue. He propped the rifle against the tree trunk and slid his parka off his right arm and then peeled the sleeve off his left arm, doing his best not to move it. His sweater was soaked with blood. Aimee swallowed against the nausea that rose in her throat.

"Sit," she said as evenly as she could. She took

the scissors and cut off the sleeves of his undergarment and his sweater, then removed them as carefully as she could.

"Oh, Matt. What happened? Is that a gunshot wound?"

His back was straight but his eyes were closed. "No," he muttered. "A tree branch."

"It went—" She twisted his arm slightly so she could see the underside, grimacing when he moaned. "It went all the way through?"

Don't let me hurt him. That was a wasted prayer. She had to clean and wrap his arm. Everything she did was going to hurt him.

"I've got to get your watch off." His hand was swollen and discolored, and the watchband looked unbearably tight. "Please, believe me. I don't want to hurt you, but it's got to come off."

It wasn't easy, and Matt was wheezing in pain by the time she was done, but she got the watch unfastened. She put it on her wrist and buckled it in the last hole.

"Aimee—" he gasped. "Before you—get started, hand me the rifle."

"It's right next to you—" She stopped as understanding dawned. He knew where it was. He just couldn't lean over to get it. Every bit of strength he had was devoted to keeping himself upright. She couldn't imagine what it had cost him to ask her to pick up the rifle and put it in his hand. She grabbed it and held it so he could get his right arm around it and his finger on the trigger.

"Thanks," he breathed.

"I don't have anything to give you for pain," she said as she sat back down and gently touched his arm.

"Just hurry."

As quickly and as gently as she could, she poured alcohol over the top of his arm and caught it with gauze pads underneath. She cleaned both awful, gaping wounds as well as she could, doing her best to ignore Matt's harsh breathing and frequent grunts of pain. By the time she was done, sweat was beading on her forehead and he had gone quiet.

"I don't know how doctors do this," she muttered as she squeezed antibiotic ointment onto a clean gauze pad and applied it to the upper wound, then did the same with the wound on the underside of his arm. Then she took a roll of gauze and wrapped it around his arm.

"Is that too tight?" she asked.

Matt's head raised a bit and he carefully moved his fingers. "No," he said shortly.

She secured the ends of the gauze with adhesive tape. When she finished, she straightened and examined his face. His skin looked tight and drawn across his cheekbones. His mouth was compressed into a thin line, and his nostrils and the corners of his lips were white and pinched. Sweat glistened on his forehead and neck.

"I'm done," she said. "Are you okay?"

"—will be."

She took a last gauze pad and wiped his face and neck, noticing that he was trembling.

"Okay, I've got something for you." She pulled out a self-heating container of hot chocolate. "I found it in one of the cupboards." Pressing a button on the bottom, she activated the chemical reaction in the container's sleeve that heated the chocolate drink inside.

"In a couple of minutes this is going to be hot chocolate. You need to drink it."

"We need to go."

"No. You're not going anywhere until you drink this." She waited until the container felt warm in her hands. Then she opened it and pressed it firmly into his right hand. "Drink."

"You need—"

"Listen, Matthew Parker. I haven't been out in the snow all night, and I didn't just single-handedly save a helpless infant. And I haven't lost pints of blood. That chocolate's all yours. Besides, I had some already. I'm full." She didn't miss his sidelong glance. She was lying, and he knew it.

Even though nothing but the nylon shell of her parka was touching the shoulder of his sweater, she felt the shudder that wracked him as he swallowed the hot, sweet liquid. Something shook loose inside her, and tears filled her eyes. Strangely, that had been happening a lot the past few days. She knew what Matt would say—probably what most people would say. *Your child's been kidnapped. It's natural to cry.*

But that wasn't true—not for her. She'd decided a long time ago that for her, crying equaled losing control. For her entire adult life, she'd prided herself on never crying. All those times when control had slipped through her fingers, leaving her feeling helpless and impotent—her parents' deaths, Will's illness and tragic death, even William's kidnapping—at least she could say she hadn't cried.

Ever since she and Matt had joined together to rescue William, she'd begun to think of crying differently. Yes, it was messy and made her feel awful, but she was seeing tears as equating more with relief and joy and even sadness than with weakness. Right now her tears represented a poignant concern for Matt, a vast relief that William was safe, and a deep-seated satisfaction that she was finally able to give Matt a fraction of the help he'd given her. She only hoped the energy in the chocolate drink would be enough to carry him to the rendezvous point. She watched him to make sure he drank every drop.

～

Mat's first swallow of hot chocolate had spread through him like a flame of desire. As soon as it hit his stomach, however, a deep, bone-rattling shudder had wracked his body. Partly a result of the hot liquid flowing through his chilled body, warming his insides. But also the clenching response of his empty stomach suddenly being hit with the hot, sugary substance. Once the initial queasiness passed, he actually felt a little better. The unrelenting pain in his arm was the same, but each throb didn't plaster black-edged stars before his eyes or trigger his gag reflex.

"Why don't you eat an energy bar?" Aimee said. "I've got several."

He squeezed his eyes shut and moved his head a fraction in a negative direction. He knew his gut wouldn't accept the chewy, fiber-rich bar. "We need to get going." He stood. For a second, the black-edged stars blinded him, so he stood still, waiting for them to fade. He wasn't going to get far if the pain in his arm kept up. Just standing jarred it.

Aimee picked up his parka but he stopped her. "I need you to do something else for me," he said.

Aimee looked up at him. "Anything," she said.

"Do you have any more tape or gauze?"

She looked into the bag. "Both, why? Are you hurt somewhere else?"

"I need you to immobilize my arm against my torso. If it starts bleeding again, I'll probably pass out, so I need to keep it as still as possible."

Aimee retrieved the scissors, but Matt shook his head. "Cut the sweater off but just wrap the gauze around the undershirt," he said, breathing harshly.

She wrapped the gauze until his forearm was sealed against his torso.

"Now help me get the parka on." Once she had his parka around his left arm and zipped, he finally lifted his head cautiously, steeling himself against nausea and dizziness. A flicker of light caught the edge of his vision. He squinted in that direction, but didn't see anything except snow drifts and fallen trees. Was it his weakness, playing visual tricks on him?

He moved his head back and forth, trying to catch the reflection again. It could have been a piece of ice that caught the sun just right, or a tiny scrap of metal turned up by the snow. Or it could have been something more ominous, like sunlight reflecting off binoculars—or the barrel of a gun.

"Do you need to rest for a little while longer?"

"No," he said, rubbing his temple with his right hand. If Al Hamir was watching them, he didn't want him to think he'd spotted him. He certainly did not want Aimee to know his suspicion. She wouldn't be able to keep from looking behind them, and that could be fatal. He was still counting on Al Hamir needing him alive. All he had to do was make sure the terrorist couldn't get a clear shot at Aimee.

The only way he could do that was to stay so close to her that Al Hamir couldn't shoot her without the risk of hitting him.

"I need something else," Matt said.

Aimee looked at him in surprise. "Sure. What do you need?"

"I need to lean on you." He held up Kinnard's rifle. "Hook the rifle over my right shoulder. Then I'm going to put my arm around your shoulders, just to keep me steady."

AIMEE BIT the inside of her cheek, doing her best not to cry. She knew he hated asking her for help. "No problem," she said, putting a false brightness into her voice. "I might even get the chance to cop a feel." She stepped in close enough to him so he could put his arm around her shoulders. "Can I put my arm around your waist without hurting you too much?"

Matt's breathing was fast and short. "I'd be—insulted if you—didn't."

Gingerly, she slid her hand under his parka and wrapped it around his middle, feeling the hard muscles of his back. Even covered by layers of clothes, they felt like long straps of steel. It terrified her how frail and breakable the human body was. Not many hours ago, his lean, rock-hard body had covered hers, strong, demanding, and unbearably sexy as they'd made love. A thrill tightened her stomach at the memory. It seemed unreal now, like a fantasy, or a dream. It was a moment stolen out of time.

This was the reality. Matt injured, needing her support. Although the arm clutching her shoulders was corded with muscles, he leaned on her heavily, needing her more at this moment than she needed him. It took a long time to figure out how to walk with Matt so close to her. Finally, once they found a rhythm, it seemed as if he were hardly leaning on her at all.

Aimee looked at Matt's watch on her wrist. It was almost two o'clock. She'd been denying the truth for over an hour. The fact was that Matt was getting weaker—much weaker. After he'd drunk the chocolate, he'd started out walking strongly, barely even resting his arm on her shoulder, but the further they went, the heavier he got. He was losing strength fast. She'd tried to get him to stop and eat something, but he'd refused. She'd forced him to drink a few of sips of water, but the last two times she'd held the bottle for him, he'd shaken his head doggedly and refused.

She was pretty sure her makeshift bandage had stemmed the flow of blood, but not in time. She knew he'd lost too much already. She knew very little about blood loss or first aid, but it made sense that if he was losing blood, he should be drinking water. "Matt, here. Have some more water."

He shook his head. "Not now," he whispered. It was the same answer he'd given the last two times she'd asked.

He turned his head to look behind them, as he'd done a number of times. Even though he hadn't said anything, she knew what he was doing. He was worried that someone was behind them, following them. "I know someone is following us," she said.

He didn't comment, but she felt a deep breath shudder through him. "It's the terrorist, isn't it? You told me you found Kinnard dead, so it's got to be Al —Al—?"

"Al Hamir."

"So how do you want to handle him? Just keep ignoring him? We should be getting close to the rendezvous point, shouldn't we?"

He nodded. "Half a mile—maybe." His voice was nothing more than a raspy whisper.

Half a mile. They'd only come three-fourths of the way? It felt like they'd been walking for hours. Matt sounded so weak it made her want to cry. But crying wouldn't accomplish anything. He'd been so strong for her. It was her turn to be strong for him. She stopped. "Matt. A half mile isn't so far. We've got a little time, and I'm not taking another step until you drink some water. You of all people should know that if you're losing blood, you should be drinking water." She uncapped the bottle and held it out. "Drink," she commanded.

He took the plastic bottle, but all he did was fill his mouth. He acted like it was agony to swallow.

"Are you nauseated? I don't have any crackers. Do you want another hot chocolate?" She tried to give him a smile. "It'll do you good."

He shook his head and swallowed the mouthful of water with difficulty. Then he blew out a hard breath, as if the mere act of swallowing had exhausted him. His face was still that scary gray color. And she knew gray-tinged skin was not a good sign. He wasn't going to make it. As soon as that thought crossed her mind, her brain screamed in protest. *No!* Matt couldn't be dying.

The water bottle fell from his hands.

"Oh, no. That's all we've got!" Aimee let go of Matt and reached for the bottle, which had rolled away. The water represented his life to her. If she could get him to drink the water, he'd be okay.

"Aimee!" Matt rasped.

She grabbed the bottle. "We only lost a little bit. It's still half full." She turned, holding the bottle up.

But Matt had gone down on one knee. His head was bent and as she watched, the rifle slipped from his shoulder. "Matt! I am so sorry." She stood.

He lifted his head. "Get down!" he yelled hoarsely. "Now!"

She dove for the ground, her hands plowing snow in front of her. Then she heard the gunshot.

CHAPTER 14

MATT HEARD the bullet whiz by his ear. His entire body clenched at the sound of the shot. Ignoring the pain that throbbed through his injured arm, he grabbed the strap of Kinnard's rifle and crawled toward the pile of snow that marked where Aimee had landed.

"Aimee," he whispered desperately. "Are you okay?" He saw the top of her head.

"Keep down," he warned, expecting another shot at any second. He slithered like a snake across the melting snow until he was close to her. Then he flipped around, so he was facing the shooter. He was going to have a hell of a time shooting with only one arm, but he could do it if he had to. Aimee was in danger. He had to. Lifting his head up over the top of the snow, he scanned the clearing, but didn't see anything.

"Matt?"

"Don't move." He knew he could outwait the other man. It would be hell to lie in wet snow with the pain in his arm stealing his breath and his fingers going numb again, but he was only minutes from getting Aimee to safety. He'd waited in colder and worse conditions than this. He could do it. He wasn't about to give up now. Clammy sweat stung his eyes and rolled down his neck. His empty stomach cramped, sending nausea crawling up his throat.

There. A flash of sun on metal. He lifted the rifle with his right hand and looked through the scope, but he couldn't focus. His eyes were blurry. He lowered the rifle and bent his head to wipe his eyes on his sleeve, but his sleeve was wet.

"Here," Aimee said. From somewhere, she pulled a dry piece of cloth and handed it to him. He wiped his eyes and face. She took the cloth back. "Can I help you hold the rifle? I could lie down and you could prop it on my back."

Matt barely heard her. Something else had grabbed his attention. He cocked his head and listened. He wasn't sure if he could trust his ears. He'd already found out he couldn't completely trust his eyes. He rolled onto his right shoulder and looked up. He had heard the rhythmic whup-whup of helicopter blades.

Aimee followed his gaze. She gasped. "Matt! Is it Deke?"

Without waiting for him to answer, she waved her arms. "He's here! Deke!" she cried.

"Aimee, don't!" His left arm jerked, an instinctive move to try and grab her. He couldn't stop an involuntary cry. He sucked in breath.

"He sees us." Just as she pulled her arms down, another shot rang out. She shrieked, grabbing her hand.

Matt pushed himself up onto his right elbow. "Aimee! Are you hit?"

She looked at her hand. "I felt something hot, but I don't see anything."

"Give me your hand." He examined it closely. There was a tiny red scrape along the flesh of her palm below her little finger. "Looks like the bullet skimmed the edge of your hand."

He closed his eyes for a second, willing away the dizziness and blurred vision. Then he glared at her. "Could you please stay still and do what I tell you?"

She bit her lip, and her cheeks turned pink. "Yes, sir," she whispered.

"Bastard's desperate. He knows once Deke lands he's got no chance to kill you or capture me." He raised his head again, scanning the area for the shooter.

"We've got to stay down until Deke lands," he

told Aimee. "If Al Hamir starts shooting at the helicopter, Deke will have to abort."

"Abort?"

Matt nodded grimly. "He can't afford to lose the helicopter. But don't worry. He's got a high-powered rifle on board. Maybe even a machine gun. He'll be back, loaded for bear."

She nodded, but her eyes were wide with fear.

"Our job is to stay down until he can put down. If I can, I'm going to take out Al Hamir if he tries to shoot the helicopter. I'd like to take the son of a bitch alive, but that may not be possible. The most important thing is to get you out of here."

"No," she snapped. "The most important thing is to get you on that helicopter and to a hospital. I'll take my chances."

Matt felt his chapped, cracked lips widen in a smile. It hurt, but he didn't care. He raised his brows. "You'll take your chances . . ."

Her cheeks got pinker, but she lifted her chin. "That's right. In fact, why don't you give me that rifle and I'll take care of Al Hamir, or whatever his name is."

The terrorist was shooting again, this time at the helicopter. Over the sound of the rotors, Matt heard the zing of a bullet ricocheting off metal. Deke took the bird up a few dozen feet, but he didn't turn away. Matt squinted up at him. "Come on, Cunningham. Don't be stupid."

"What? What's the matter?"

"Deke's drawing his fire." Matt swiped his forehead on the sleeve of his parka again and flipped over onto his stomach, suppressing a groan.

"Why?"

Matt swallowed the bile that was threatening to erupt from his throat. He felt like he was about to puke his guts up. The good news was that his arm had quit hurting. It was just numb. Or was that the bad news? Pushing away those thoughts, he lifted the rifle and sighted through the scope. "He knows our terrorist friend's got to come out from his cover to get a shot at him. He's drawing him out so I can shoot him." He blew out a harsh breath. "I hope I can."

Aimee scooted over closer to him. "Matt, lean on me. Use me to brace the gun."

Matt's right arm was shaking with fatigue and weakness from loss of blood. He shook his head. "What are you talking about?"

"Here. Move over." She crawled around until her body was perpendicular to his. "Let me lie in front of you, and you can brace the gun on my back. Won't that work?"

He didn't want to tell her that most of what she'd just said sounded like gibberish to his buzzing ears. He just watched as she lay flat on her stomach in front of him. "Now, brace the barrel of the rifle on me."

Slowly, his brain processed her words. "Maybe," he whispered. "I can try."

"Listen," Aimee said. "Deke's coming lower. Al Hamir will probably shoot at him." She took a long breath. "Get ready."

Matt set the barrel of the rifle across her shoulders and pushed himself forward until he could see through the scope. "Aimee?"

"Yeah?"

He blinked sweat out of his eyes, and swept the scope back and forth, looking for the terrorist. "I love you."

Her body stiffened, making the scope wobble. "Hey," he muttered. "Stay still. I almost had him."

"Are you okay?" she asked, a worried tone in her voice. "Please be okay."

"Hold still." He concentrated all the energy he had left in him on watching through the scope. Then he saw him. Al Hamir. He'd slipped out from behind a tree to get a shot at Deke. He'd braced himself and was aiming at the helicopter that loomed over their heads. "Don't move. I've got him," Matt whispered. His vision wavered, but hell, it was a short shot. The guy was presenting a perfect target, the way he stood with his feet apart. It was a sucker shot.

Slowly, carefully, Matt squeezed the trigger. He saw the man jerk, saw blood blossom on the leg of his pants. As he watched, the terrorist dropped to his knees. Then he turned the rifle on Matt. For an instant, they were scope-to-scope, but then Al Hamir shifted his barrel downward. He was going to shoot Aimee. Matt pulled the trigger again and again and again. The last thing he remembered was a burst of bright stars before his eyes.

THE CLEAN WHITE sheets and pillow felt like heaven to Aimee's exhausted muscles and chapped skin. Even the cotton hospital gown couldn't have felt better if it were the finest silk. Better than all that was the tiny bundle that was nestled into the curve of her arm.

She looked down at William. He was asleep. He'd seemed singularly unconcerned that she'd been gone. As soon as she'd stopped kissing him all over his face and touching every tiny perfect finger and toe, he'd fallen right to sleep.

"Must be nice," she murmured drowsily, "to be so sure that everything's fine in your world." She chuckled softly.

The nurse, who'd been watching them, spoke. "All right, Mrs. Vick. It's time for William to go back to his crib. He'll soon be ready for some more food, but for now you should take a nap."

Reluctantly, Aimee let the nurse take her baby out of her arms. A frisson of fear crawled up her spine, but that was just a reflex. She knew they were both safe.

"Bye bye, William Matthew," she whispered. "I think they gave me something to make me sleepy. I'm just going to take a little nap. Then when I wake up, you and I can go find Matt." Her heart gave a slight jump. Deke had told her Matt was going to be fine. Hadn't he? Her eyes drifted closed. Or had she dreamed it? She didn't remember much after Deke and Brock got them into the helicopter. Just Deke's deep, reassuring voice, saying everything was going to be all right. But what else was he going to say in that situation? *Sorry guys, looks like you're not going to make it?*

Deke had landed the helicopter on the roof of the hospital and all kinds of excitement had broken out. Men and women dressed in blue with rolling tables had rushed out, bracing against the down-wind from the rotors, and grabbed Matt.

Aimee remembered trying to see where they took him, but more people ran out and grabbed her. Somebody leaned over her and said something, and that was all she remembered until she woke up while a nurse's aide was bathing her. The nurse could tell her about Matt. She reached for the call button, but her arm was tired and her eyelids were heavy. "In a minute," she whispered.

MATT JERKED. The terrorist! He was shooting at Aimee! Matt tried to pull the trigger, but he couldn't. Something was wrong with his hand.

He opened his eyes. All he saw was blue and white. Blue walls, low blue light. White sheets. *Sheets?* He looked down at himself. He was covered up to his chest by a white sheet. His left arm was wrapped up like a mummy, and his right arm was strapped down, with tubes running in several different directions.

What the hell? He felt drugged. Very drugged. Like he'd felt years ago when he'd woken up from an emergency appendectomy. His eyes burned and his mouth was dry, but not as dry as it had been. His arm hurt, but not as badly as it had before. Before what? Closing his eyes, he tried to wipe his mind free of all the confusing and disturbing images that were clicking through it like a slideshow gone out of control.

—Aimee, lying so close to the spreading pool of gasoline.

—Kinnard pointing that assault rifle at her.

—His own arm impaled by a piece of wood.

—Kinnard's girlfriend jerking when the bullet hit her head.

—Brock hauling up the basket carrying its precious cargo.

Matt growled and opened his eyes. Closing them had only sped up the slideshow. He stared at the ceiling, counting off the pictures as they flashed across his inner vision, trying to pick out the latest ones and shuffle them into some sort of order.

He remembered Aimee waving at Deke. He remembered her lying down in front of him so he could use her as a prop for the rifle barrel. He remembered pulling the trigger again and again and again. For the life of him, he couldn't remember anything after that. What a weakling he was. Some rescuer he was. It was pretty bad when the rescuer had to be rescued. It was a good thing Deke was there, because if it had been left up to him, Aimee would probably be dead now.

Aimee. He had to find her—check on her. He looked around for the nurse call button and discovered someone had had the foresight to put it next to his right hand. With more effort than he'd have thought he'd need, he lifted his hand enough to get his finger on the button and pressed it.

—help you?

"Get me a nurse now!" What he heard in his ears was nothing like what he'd intended. He'd barked a command, but a raspy whisper was all that had come out of his mouth. The very act of punching the button and speaking had started his heart to hammering and his head to pounding. He closed his eyes and pretended the dampness that leaked out from under his lids wasn't tears.

"Mr. Parker, are you all right?"

He turned his head enough to see the pretty young woman dressed in some kind of smock with dogs and cats on it. "Get me unhooked from all this stuff. I've got to check on Aimee."

The young woman smiled as she stepped over to the bed and patted his hand. "I'm glad to see you're awake and feeling better, but you won't be able to get up for a while. You've only been out of the recovery room for an hour or so."

"Recovery room?"

"The surgery on your arm." She punched some buttons on the monitor that was beeping behind his head, and checked the bag of fluid that hung on a pole beside him. "Everything looks good. You have some visitors who have been waiting for you to wake up. They're down in the coffee shop. I'll call them, and in a few minutes, I'll bring you a sleeping pill."

"Visitors? Is it Aimee?"

"Aimee? The woman who was brought in with you? No." She pulled off gloves he hadn't noticed she had on and pumped a bit of antiseptic gel on her hands from a dispenser hanging on the wall.

"Wait a minute. Where am I?"

She pointed at a white board hanging on the wall directly across from his bed, where the name of the hospital, the date, and the names of his nurses and aides were written. "You're in Crook County Hospital. Today is Monday, barely, and my name is Kinsey. I'll be back soon."

Matt studied the tubes and needles that were sticking out of his right hand, trying to decide how much it would hurt to pull them out. He wanted to look closer at them but for some reason he found it very hard to lift his arm. He turned his attention to his other arm. He still had his hand. It was sticking out from the huge roll of bandages. It looked swollen and discolored, but at least it was there. Before he had a chance to wonder what the surgeons had done to it, the room door opened and Irina came in, followed by Brock and FBI Special Agent Schiff.

"Matt! Oh my goodness, you look awful!" Irina laughed self-consciously as she stepped around to the far side of the bed and patted his hand. "I mean, you look wonderful, given all that you've been through. How are you feeling?"

Brock nodded and scowled as if he were irritated to see Matt alive. But Matt knew that was his usual expression, so he merely nodded back. "Where's Aimee?" he asked Irina.

"She and William are doing fine. Aimee's been admitted overnight, but they should be able to go home tomorrow." Irina looked at Special Agent Schiff.

He stepped forward. "Sorry, but we need to talk to you."

Matt ignored him. "Irina," he rasped. "Aimee can't go home by herself. She's been through too much. Can you do something? She shouldn't go back to Margo's house."

"Don't worry. We're going to take good care of her." She picked up the cup of water and held the straw to his lips. He took a couple of swallows and coughed.

"Margo Vick won't be going anywhere near Aimee," Schiff said. "Not any time soon. I can promise you that."

"What are you talking about?"

"Once we found out that the baby was being held at the Vick's hunting cabin, we got a warrant for Mrs. Vick's financial and telephone records, and her home. We found that a hundred thousand dollars had been transferred from Mrs. Vick's account to a numbered account overseas within the past week. Mrs. Vick and her accountant claim to know nothing about it. There were also two calls to Mrs. Vick's home telephone from a survivalist group of which Kinnard is a member."

"Was a member," Matt said.

Schiff nodded.

The FBI Agent pulled his phone from his pocket and made a quick note, then continued. "The telephone calls from the survivalist group to Mrs.

Vick's number were short, less than a minute. Mrs. Vick stated that she received a couple of calls in the past week where she was asked to hold. She said she held for a short while, and then hung up."

Matt cut his eyes over at the FBI agent. "It's possible she was framed."

"I know. It's beginning to look that way."

That surprised Matt. He lifted his head and immediately regretted it. The movement hurt his arm and he felt queasy. "What do you mean?" he asked softly.

"We picked up the body of the man you shot. Cunningham gave us the coordinates. He was carrying a cell phone, with a message from an unidentified number. The message was in Arabic. We got it translated. Basically, it said—" Schiff looked back at his phone. "Kill kidnappers. No survivors to identify us."

Matt's pulse jumped. "The kidnapper was hired by Novus, too."

"Novus?" Schiff frowned. "The terrorist Novus Ordo?" He turned to glare at Irina. When he did, Brock took a step closer to her.

Schiff addressed Irina. "I figured the dead guy might be somehow involved with the search for your husband, but *Novus Ordo?*"

Irina gazed at him evenly.

"Well, that explains a lot. Not everything, but a lot. We had the voice of the caller who set up the ransom drop analyzed. There were certain inflections and idiomatic inconsistencies that indicated that English may not have been his first language."

"May not?" Irina repeated.

Schiff nodded. "The results were inconclusive. My expert couldn't be sure. He said it was possible that the caller was trying to alter his phrasing to make us think he might not be American."

Matt closed his eyes and sighed. "So we can't prove whether the whole thing was engineered by Novus or not."

"It would help if all the people involved in the kidnapping weren't dead. Couldn't you have left one of them alive?"

"Agent Schiff," Irina broke in. "Matt needs to sleep. He's still under the effects of the anesthesia from his surgery."

Schiff sent her a sharp glance. "Fine. I'll get his statement tomorrow, when he's feeling better. Mrs. Castle, may I speak to you after we're done here?"

She glanced at Matt. "Yes, of course."

"Irina, what about—what about the sabotage?" Matt whispered.

Irina leaned over. "We'll talk about that later," she said softly.

Just then the nurse came in. "It's time for Mr. Parker's medication."

"Don't worry about Aimee," Irina said. "I'll check on you tomorrow."

Brock hadn't said a word the entire time. In fact, he'd hardly moved, except when he'd stood between Schiff and Irina. He'd just listened intently to everything that was said. As Irina, Schiff, and Brock left the room, Brock met Matt's gaze and nodded, the scowl still on his face.

The nurse injected something into the IV tubing that ran from the bag of fluid down into his hand. "There you go, Mr. Parker." She peeled off her exam gloves, then turned and looked at him.

"Who was that man?" she asked, her eyes wide and her cheeks flushed.

"The guy in the suit?"

"No. The one with the eye patch. The dangerous looking one. Who was he?"

Matt's eyelids were getting heavy. "You mean Brock O'Neill?" he muttered. "That's a real good question. I'm not sure any of us know exactly who he is." He peered at her. "You want me to introduce you?"

She laughed and shook her head. "Oh, no. I was married to a dangerous man. I'll never make that mistake again. You get some sleep, and I'll be back later to check your vital signs."

THE DOOR to Matt's hospital room was closed. It had taken Aimee much longer than she'd anticipated to be discharged, although the doctor had promised her yesterday that he was only admitting her overnight for observation. The nurses on her floor had brought her a set of scrubs to wear and had outfitted William with clothes from the pediatric floor.

Now, finally, she was here. Brock O'Neill had shown up to escort her to Castle Ranch, and he'd wheeled them to Matt's door. Brock knocked on the door for her.

"He could be asleep," she said, feeling suddenly shy about going into his room. "Or being given a bath. Or what if he doesn't want to see me?"

"Doubt that's it," Brock muttered.

She took a deep breath. "Well, it doesn't matter, because I'm going to see him before I leave, if only for a moment." She wasn't about to leave the hospital without making sure he was okay. "If he's asleep, we'll go."

Brock stood back to allow her to enter. The room was dark. The curtains were closed. The only light came from the dim recessed fixture above the bed. Matt was asleep.

She knew she should turn around and leave, but she couldn't take her eyes off him. She'd been so afraid he wouldn't make it. They'd taken him away so fast once the helicopter had landed.

She moved carefully over to the bed, hoping that William would stay quiet. The shadows cast by the dim light emphasized the pain lines etched between Matt's brows and around his mouth. His hair was a little bit tousled, enough that she wanted to reach out and brush it back from his forehead. And his mouth was as straight and grim as it had been the last time she'd seen him, right before the emergency doctors had rolled him away.

"I'm so sorry," she mouthed, not really sure why she was apologizing. Mostly that he'd been hurt so badly for trying to help her, she supposed.

"You've got nothing to be sorry for," he whispered.

She jumped, jostling the car seat. William made a tiny noise of protest, but Aimee couldn't take her eyes off Matt. He opened his eyes, those deep, dark eyes, and looked at her.

"Matt," she breathed, her pulse hammering in her throat. "You're—okay?"

His mouth curved up slightly. "Depends on what you mean by okay. I'm here, and essentially in one piece." He lifted his right hand, which attached to what looked like a tangle of tubing, and pressed a button. The head of the bed rose up. He winced slightly, and Aimee's gaze went to his left arm, which was covered by a fat bandage. "What—what did they say about your arm?"

His long dark lashes swept downward. "The doctor came in earlier. He said all I needed to know was that they cleaned the wound, sewed some muscles and tendons back together, and stitched it all up." He looked down at the bandage. "He said it wouldn't be pretty, but with a little luck and a lot of physical therapy, it should probably work okay, thanks to whoever cleaned and bandaged it."

Aimee took a long breath. "I'm so glad."

"Me too, although I have a feeling he really meant a whole lot of luck rather than just a little." He raised his gaze to hers. "How are you? You look good."

"I'm good," she said, nodding. "I'm fine. I brought someone to see you."

"William—?" Matt's voice broke, and Aimee's heart felt like it cracked in two.

She smiled. "He wants to say thank you." She swallowed the lump that had risen in her throat.

"Let me see him."

She set the baby seat down and took William into her arms. "Can I sit down?" She nodded toward the side of his bed.

"Sure. Bring him over here."

She bounced the baby in her arms as she walked around and sat gingerly on the edge of the bed. She propped William on her lap. Matt lifted his right hand, then checked his gesture. "Think the tubes will scare him?"

As if in answer, William cooed and waved his arms.

"I don't think anything about you could possibly scare him. He's happy to see you."

"Yeah?"

"William? You know who this is, don't you? Remember Matt? He's your godfather. He saved you."

"Aimee, don't—" Matt's hand fell back to the bed.

"Don't what? Tell my son the truth? You did save him. You saved him and me."

Matt leaned his head back and closed his eyes. "If you're going to tell him the truth, tell him the whole truth. Tell him what happened to his father. Tell him that I didn't have the sense or the courage to refuse to take Will skydiving. I didn't have the good sense to make him take some practice runs or do a buddy-dive."

"Will had skydived before. His carelessness wasn't your responsibility."

Matt blinked. "What? Why have you suddenly changed your mind?"

"Changed my mind? What are you talking about?"

"Are you feeling sorry for me? Is that it? What happened to blaming me for letting Will die?"

"I never blamed you."

"Hah." He squeezed his eyes shut and shook his head. "I saw how you looked at me when I brought him home."

"Matt, I can't remember what I did or said or even thought that night. What I do remember is what Will always told me. *You can count on Matt.* He said that the day before you and he left on your trip. *Matt's safe as houses.*"

Matt lifted his head and looked at her. "I don't know why he thought that."

"I do, now."

He stared at her, his dark eyes glittering with unshed tears.

"It took me a while, to understand what he meant. He knew you, better than anyone. He knew you'd die, if by dying you could save an innocent life."

He shrugged and winced. "For some reason, Will always believed in me."

William was getting restless. He began to fuss. "I guess I'd better put this little guy back in his seat."

"Can I—?"

Aimee knew what Matt was trying to ask. She held William close enough that Matt could press a kiss to his fat little cheek. "Hey there, William," he whispered. "Aren't you glad to see your mom? I can promise you I am."

She turned to fasten William back into his seat.

"Aimee?"

She didn't look up. She was busy blinking away the tears that she couldn't stop. Seeing Matt kissing her little boy had shattered the last fragile pieces of her heart.

"Aimee—"

She lifted her head without really looking at him. "I'm listening. I just need to get William Matthew settled."

"Could you—maybe one day—give me a chance?"

She froze for an instant, wondering if she'd heard what she thought she had. She tested the last strap, to be sure William was safe in his seat.

Slowly, she raised her gaze to his. "Give you a chance?"

The muscles of his jaw worked. "I—" he swallowed. "I love you."

She gasped softly. "You said that before. I thought you were hallucinating."

He shook his head. "I wasn't hallucinating." Then his gaze wavered. She'd seen him face killer snowstorms, assault rifles, gasoline fires, and a horrible injury, but this was the first time she'd seen him nearly paralyzed with fear.

Her mouth stretched into a grin, even as fat tears slipped from her eyes and plopped onto her hands. "I am—so glad," she said, her voice shaking with sobs. "Because I wasn't sure how I was going to—tell you that I fell in—love with you the minute you pressured me into letting you go with me."

"You did?" he said, his brows shooting up.

"Well, it didn't hurt that you made the supreme sacrifice of warming me with your own naked body."

"Any time," he said.

"Promise?" she said with a little smile.

"I promise. You—?" he paused. "You're okay with me being William's stepfather? I mean—are you saying you'll—you know?"

"I have something to tell you. When Will found out he had cancer, he made me promise him something."

"Yeah? What?" Matt still looked scared.

"He made me promise that when I was ready, I'd think about you first." She'd done pretty well so far, but remembering Will's words and thinking how prophetic they were, she looked at the man she knew would always keep his promises. Love and desire welled up inside her and pushed away the last bits of the control she'd always clung to like a lifeline. For the first time in her life, she broke down and sobbed.

Matt lifted his hand. "Aimee, are you okay?"

"Sure." She sniffed.

"You're crying."

"I know," she wailed.

Matt's mouth curved into a smile. "Does that mean this qualifies as a special occasion?"

She leaned over and kissed him on the mouth as tears streamed down her face. "I think it qualifies as the first in a lifetime of amazingly special occasions."

THE END

COMING SOON
THE TROUBLE WITH DEKE
BLACK HILLS BROTHERHOOD – BOOK TWO
BROTHERHOOD PROTECTORS WORLD

FORMER AIR FORCE COMBAT Rescue Officer Deke Cunningham has never met an opponent he couldn't beat. But when the love of his life left him, it took him a long time to recover. An unexpected night of passion with her sent him back to square one, so he fought his way back again. Now Mindy has been taken hostage by terrorists to lure him into a trap. He can't refuse, but he'll be damned if he'll fall under her spell again.

MINDY NEVER WANTED Deke to know they'd conceived a baby on that careless night. She's prepared to rear the child alone. Now she's not sure who she'd rather face—the terrorists holding her or Deke when he sees she's eight-months pregnant.

. . .

DEKE AND MINDY are prey in a dark and deadly underground maze. Deke could easily handle these guys alone, but he's responsible for Mindy's safety, too. How in hell will he get them out of this mess? And *if* he can save her and their unborn baby, what's he going to do then?

Historical Romance

September Rain

The Christmas Treasure

Anthologies & Short Stories

Silk and Magic: Book One

The Journey Home

Three Christmases: A Short Story

Bestselling romance author Mallory Kane has published over 40 romantic suspense titles between Harlequin Intrigue and Tule Publishing Group, and she has multiple independent projects spanning genres. Mallory loves romantic suspense with dangerous heroes and dauntless heroines, and she enjoys tossing in a bit of her medical knowledge for an extra dose of intrigue.

Mallory taught herself to read at age three, starting a lifelong love affair with books. Her mother, a librarian, loved and respected books and taught Mallory that they were a precious resource. Her father was a brilliant storyteller. His oral histories are chronicled in such places as the Veterans' History Project at the Library of Congress. He was always her biggest fan.

When she's not writing, Mallory enjoys designing one-of-a-kind jewelry using broken vintage pieces and creating collaged greeting cards. She lives in

East Tennessee with her husband, Michael, and their cats, Dusty and Smoke Monster.

Mallory loves hearing from her readers. Connect with her on Facebook, Goodreads, BookBub, her website, or via email at mallory@mallorykane.com.

facebook.com/AuthorMalloryKane
bookbub.com/profile/mallory-kane

Hot SEAL Bachelor Party (SEALs in Paradise)

ABOUT ELLE JAMES

ELLE JAMES also writing as MYLA JACKSON is a *New York Times* and *USA Today* Bestselling author of books including cowboys, intrigues and paranormal adventures that keep her readers on the edges of their seats. With over eighty works in a variety of sub-genres and lengths she has published with Harlequin, Samhain, Ellora's Cave, Kensington, Cleis Press, and Avon. When she's not at her computer, she's traveling, snow skiing, boating, or riding her ATV, dreaming up new stories. Learn more about Elle James at www.ellejames.com

Website | Facebook | Twitter | GoodReads | Newsletter | BookBub | Amazon

Follow Elle!
www.ellejames.com
ellejames@ellejames.com

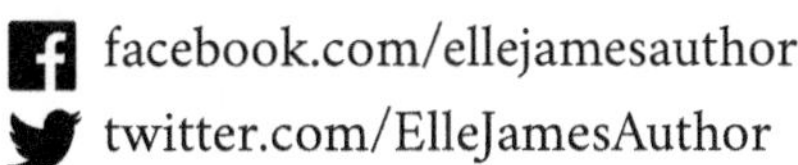
facebook.com/ellejamesauthor
twitter.com/ElleJamesAuthor